The Bigfoot Runes

as told to
Rusty Wilson

PREFACE

by Rusty Wilson

Is this story true? This is the first question I'm always asked by readers, and I have to answer—I don't know.

Was there really a man named Sam who told it to me? Yes, that part is true, but if he was just making it up or not, only he knows. But if he was, he's a very convincing story-teller. And I have seen the drawing of the Bigfoot above his hearth and it is also quite convincing.

Regardless, it's a unique and interesting story, and one I think you'll find is about much more than just Bigfoot, but also about our place in the natural world, as well as about questioning things we often take for granted.

The backstory was told in my book, "Rusty Wilson's Bigfoot Campfire Stories," but you don't need to read that to understand, as enough is told here to fill you in. And the afterword to this story by Professor Johnson will add even more detail.

Anyway, this story was told to me by Sam (Packy) during a number of evenings next to a warm fireplace in the little town of Fernie in British Columbia, Canada, where I recorded it, later turning it into this book, pretty much word for word. I've changed some of the names and places for reasons of anonymity.

Since I'm known for my Bigfoot stories, Sam had contacted me, asking me to come visit, saying he had a story I might like to hear. And in retrospect, I feel honored that he chose me for its telling.

I hope you, my fellow adventurers, enjoy it as much as I have.

Best wishes,
Rusty Wilson

The
Bigfoot
Runes

Flattops

Coffee Pot Springs

Rune Cave

Girl Scout Camp

Glenwood Springs

Grand Junction

Green River

Utah

Colorado

N
NW NE
W E
SW SE
S

Caution: Map drawn to Bigfoot scale.

CHAPTER 1

Rusty, you ask why I went back to the Rune Cave—well, I don't know why. I've spent many hours contemplating that question, and I'm no closer to an answer than when I actually did go back.

I asked myself, over and over, as I was driving up the road to Coffeepot Springs, why are you doing this? It might very easily mean the end of your life. Being killed by a Bigfoot is probably about like being killed by a grizzly bear, and we've all heard the horrors of that story.

I even laughed a bit at myself for believing in Bigfoot, but I knew what I'd seen in the drawing in the Book of Runes. There was no other name for it but Bigfoot—unless maybe the word insanity.

But nothing could stop me from returning. Ever since I'd first seen the Book of Runes, I had to return. It was like a compulsion, something I had no control over, even though it might mean my death. I had dreams about it, it wouldn't leave me alone, so I went back.

When I did finally go back, it was late spring, and there had just been a storm go through, which left a bit of snow up there on top. As I parked my old pickup at the springs, I wondered if I shouldn't leave a note so people would know what happened, why the owner of the truck never returned.

That old truck was eventually hauled off to the sheriff's compound as possible evidence in a missing person's case, and I was that missing person, but I sure wasn't missing in the way I would've predicted.

I wasn't killed by a Bigfoot, obviously, or I wouldn't be here pondering the question of why I went back. But I did go missing, and I would remain so for a long time.

Sometimes I wonder what it would be like if I was still out there, missing, but I had to come back to civilization—I had no choice, really, after it was all said and done.

But it was OK, I'd already been missing for years. The real me had died long ago, or gone into hibernation. I'd forgotten pretty much who I was, and all I knew was that I was tired of being in pain, and somehow the Book of Runes had the key to finding myself again. How, I had no idea. I just knew I had to go back to the cave. There was something about that book that spelled hope for me—maybe a last-chance kind of hope.

When I first found the book there deep in the cave, I took photos of it, of every damn page, with my little pocket digital camera, even though I was literally shaking in fear. I knew even then that the book had something I needed. I took the photos of the book to Professor Johnson, and I hoped that would be the end of it.

The prof was all excited about it, and I figured if anyone could make sense of it, it was him. He was a pretty famous linguist—that's why I took it to him. I painstakingly took a picture of each page of that dang book, as well as of the runes that lined the cave, then I had to leave. I somehow knew I would be killed if I was found there with the book.

At first, I wanted to know what the prof came up with. I was intrigued by it all, and who wouldn't be? How often does someone find a book like that in a cave? I eventually thought about it and figured there would be money to be made—but that wasn't what motivated me, I was simply curious.

But then, as time passed, I lost interest in the translation, and I wanted to know more about the ones who the book belonged to. I began to feel a sense of violation.

What right did I have to take photos of this book and show them around? It wasn't mine to do that with, and I started feeling guilty. I wanted the prof to drop the whole thing, but by then, I was out in the backcountry and had no way of getting ahold of him. He'd given me a cellphone, but I'd lost it somewhere on the road.

But man, that book was something else. It was big, and it sat on a pedestal in the cave, a stand made of deer antlers. It was all handmade, you could tell. And what was really spooky was the cave it was in—the runes carved all around the entrance and on the inside wall where the book sat. That was really something that took some time and work.

The book's cover was some kind of leather, and you could see it had been chewed to make it soft. And the paper, well, it looked like the same deal, like someone had chewed on some kind of plants and made them all soft and then rolled them out like pie dough to dry.

The pages were a soft greenish color, and the runes inscribed on them were made with some kind of stick using a dark pigment. I would guess some kind of iron-based pigment, as they were black with a tinge of red to them. Hematite, maybe.

3

See, I know hematite. I may come across as uneducated, but I used to be a geologist, back before I got so lost. But when I went into the military, well, that put an end to it all.

Ironic as hell, a scientist hooking up with a Bigfoot, the stuff of myth and legend—and nightmares.

When I went into the war, I was a medic. I ended up being a damn good medic, and I saved a lot of lives, but it was the ones I didn't save that about killed me. I came home with PTSD and found out that nobody wanted a guy with PTSD, not even my so-called loving wife. I'd lost my innocence, my optimism and faith in humans, and my mind wouldn't stay still.

I couldn't find a job, and I ended up with a small pension from the Army for the PTSD, so I started living in the back of my old truck out in the wilds. That's how it all started. And the more I was out there, the less I wanted anything to do with civilization.

But back to this Book of Runes. I had no idea what was in it, what the message was, but I knew it had something for me. I suspected it laid out a whole new kind of living that I knew nothing about, and I wanted and needed a new life.

But there was something more—I knew the Bigfoot were onto something I needed to survive, to begin to wake up and live my life again. I was desperate.

So I went back to the Rune Cave. The irony of it all was, what I was looking for wasn't in the book at all, but came from the Bigfoot themselves—and from within me.

So, I had no choice but to go back.

And I also know I need to tell you this story because maybe it will help someone else. So, let's get started.

CHAPTER 2

So, I went back to the Rune Cave. I parked my old truck by the springs, then hiked up to that cave in a state of pure suspense and fear, fear worse than any battle I'd been in, and the tension was crazy.

I was on pins and needles, and I kept asking myself why I was doing this—something kept telling me to turn around and get the hell out of there, but I ignored it.

I finally came to the cave and hid there behind the trees and just watched and listened for at least an hour. You might say I was working up the courage to go inside.

I was wanting to go inside, but I was also wanting to stay alive. See, there was a drawing in the book, and if it was indicative of who that book belonged to, well, I sure as hell didn't want to meet up with them.

And that drawing was something else. It was a very well done sketch of these two dark figures that were very muscular, with wide shoulders and broad faces—faces that looked almost human, very intelligent.

One wore a sort of crown that looked like it was made of antlers. The other looked female—it was less massive and wore a crown made of leaves.

Both were impressive looking, with heads that came to a sort of crest or point, their shoulders melting into the

5

neck muscles. And both were covered completely with dark hair, head to toe.

Now I can look at that sketch any time I want, as it's in a frame above my fireplace, and I find it very peaceful. It reminds me of ones I really care about, though I don't get to see them very often. But then, at that time, it was terrifying.

Anyway, standing in front of that cave, I finally just gritted my teeth and went in. That strange musky smell I'd smelled before was there, only stronger than I remembered it being. That made me think that maybe they'd been in there recently, the ones who owned the book.

I knew then I was dealing with Bigfoot, but I refused to admit it to myself because it was too terrifying a thought. Besides, I didn't really even believe they existed. It had to be a hoax.

I slowly edged into the main cave, wondering what I would find. Would the book still be there? Did they somehow know that it had been touched? Could they smell my fingerprints on the pages? I knew they would be angry and kill me.

The whole thing just felt like it must be very important to them—the runes carved everywhere in the cave, the elaborate antler stand, the handmade cover and pages—all of it.

As I entered the main cave, I could see everything was just like I'd left it. I stopped and stood there for a moment, not sure what to do. Why had I come back?

I hadn't thought any of this out, and now it seemed to me that if I wanted to find any answers, I would have to take that book. But that didn't make sense, as I already had photos of all its pages—I could go visit the prof and we could decipher what was there.

There was no need to steal it, and I couldn't read it anyway, it was all written in what looked like some kind of runes. I hadn't gone back with the intention of stealing it, not at all, but that's what I now intended to do.

So, I stood there and looked at it for awhile, then I picked up the Book of Runes. It wasn't very heavy, considering how large it was, which surprised me.

I kept telling myself it was just a book—one made of paper and a leather cover—just a book. But I felt kind of electrified, standing there holding it, kind of an adrenaline rush.

I stood there, not sure what the heck I was even doing, holding that book, when I realized I was talking to myself. And then, all of a sudden, my instincts said to get out of there.

I tucked the book under my arm and started out of the cave, when suddenly, I heard a voice. It vibrated through my skull, making me want to shake my head to be rid of it.

"Give me the book. They'll kill you."

I looked around. The voice pierced through my head, yet it was different from a normal voice. It's hard to describe, but it was like it went directly into my brain. It had no bass, no tenor, no sound at all, but was like a pure light shining straight into my mind, a light that carried meaning.

I was shaking like a leaf, but I managed to reply, "No. It's mine now."

The voice replied, "I can't understand you."

"I said, I'm not giving it up," I answered, shaking in my boots.

"I can't understand you."

Now a large shadow stepped from the darkness in the back of the cave, and I was even more terrified—but I held onto that book. In retrospect, and I think about this a lot, that book seemed to me at the time to be my only lifeline. If I died trying to find its answers, so be it—I had nothing to lose anyway.

Now I could make out more than shadow, and what I saw was right from the sketches in the book, exactly what I had feared. It had to be a Bigfoot, some kind of relict human or something along another evolutionary path, but human-like.

It towered over me and was at least seven feet tall, with broad shoulders and long muscled arms that hung clear down to its knees. Its legs were like tree trunks, and its face, what I could make out, seemed human, but also ape-like with its flat nose and broad hairless cheeks.

And somehow, this beast was communicating to me without speaking. His mouth didn't move a bit, and I could understand him perfectly, but he couldn't comprehend a word I was saying.

"You must learn to thoughtcast so we can communicate. They're coming back, and they will kill you. Give me the book."

"No," I replied, holding the book close to my chest, under my jacket.

"Can you hear them coming? They're coming back into the lower chamber. They're thoughtcasting about you, wondering where you are. They saw you come up the trail. They know you're here."

I was now completely filled with the most unreasonable terror I'd ever known. The beast stepped closer to me, but he didn't act menacing. He smelled dank and musty, that same odor I noticed when I entered the cave.

He again projected meaning into my mind.

"All right. Keep the book. Follow me. Hurry. They're very angry and will kill you. It won't be a pleasant thing. We'll do this together, stubborn human."

I suddenly felt a huge hand on my shoulder, and the beast practically dragged me along with him. It was then that I knew he could easily take the book from me, like taking a toy from a small child. I knew he was showing me great respect, treating me like an equal, even as he dragged me along.

It somehow messed with my sense of human superiority, having this beast treat me like that. I knew I was terribly outgunned in size, and on top of that, this creature could somehow telepath its thoughts to me!

I somehow knew he wouldn't harm me and that I needed to do what he said—except give up the book, and no way was I going to do that.

It was my first foray into a humility that the beast engendered and that would change my life, as well as how I would come to view the world—or rather, what would become a whole new world for me.

I would later come to call him Hap, short for Happy, because he was happy, although I would never have guessed it then, as at the time, he was really upset.

So, Hap dragged me along until we came to the mouth of the cave, where we veered into the deep underbrush and began retreating from the cave's entrance as fast as we could.

CHAPTER 3

I followed Hap, running for my life, the thick underbrush whipping my face and arms, tearing my long shirt sleeves into shreds. For every three or four steps I took, Hap took one, and I could tell he was frustrated by our slow progress.

"They know where we are. They're setting up an ambush ahead," he cast.

"How do they know?" I asked.

"I can't understand you. No point trying. I'll teach you to thoughtcast later. For now, you must get on my shoulders. I can hear them casting, and they're after us. They know the book is missing."

He swept me up as if I were a rag doll and put me on his broad shoulders. I sat hunched over his huge back, one arm around where his thick shoulders met the base of his head and my other arm desperately holding onto the Book of Runes.

Hap's hair hung off his arms a good eight inches, though it was smooth and short on the rest of his body. Now that we were outside in the light, I could see he was a dark brown color and had reddish highlights on his face and chest. For some reason, I took him to be young, like a human in their 20s, in his prime.

Now Hap veered back onto the trail and turned completely around, heading back towards the cave. I had no control over where we went, but that cave was the last place I wanted to be.

But just before we came to the entrance, he turned and went down a steep rocky scree slope at an incredible speed, one I could never have kept up with, especially on that kind of an incline. It had to be a good 60 degrees or more, and I felt like I was riding on the shoulders of a giant ape— and who knows, maybe I was.

Scree flowed around his huge legs, and I worried he would take that whole steep scree field down with us. But I couldn't believe it—we were at its base before I could even process how fast we were going.

I turned and looked back up and was amazed at how steep it really was. A few loose rocks were still tumbling down, making a clattering sound.

Now Hap ducked into the thick forest and ran like the wind. I worried that I would be knocked off by a tree branch, but he seemed aware of that and often ducked and stooped to accommodate me. We weren't on any trail, just fleeing straight through the thick fir and spruce forest of the Flattop Mountains of Colorado.

I had no idea how fast we were going, but it felt like I was riding a horse at a fast gallop, or maybe even faster. It was all I could do to hang on, even though his stride was smooth, almost like he was floating. I had now again tucked the book under my jacket and zipped it up so I could hold onto Hap with both arms.

It seemed like we'd gone miles before I felt Hap's sides begin to heave a bit. I was amazed at the kind of shape he must be in. He then stopped and rested, tilting his huge head as if listening. I could hear nothing, not even the normal sounds of the forest. No birds, nothing.

Now a new thought entered my mind. "They're sending out Tracker."

I knew it came from Hap, and I swore I could feel him tremble a bit. A blackness seemed to come over him like a cloud of fear.

I said nothing, as I knew he couldn't understand me anyway. I was mystified how I could comprehend what he was telling me, but I somehow did.

Hap was soon on his way, me clinging on while he ran in a fast jog. I was amazed at his speed, especially through thick forest and rocky ledges and up and down hills. We seemed to be losing altitude, and we were soon in a drainage, following a small creek.

"I can outsmart Tracker," Hap cast. "I can run in water where he won't find my tracks."

Even though he seemed confident, I sensed a great fear had come over him.

I worried now that Hap would fall in the slippery stream, but I understood his logic. This Tracker must be a very scary thing for something as big and fierce as Hap to be afraid of it.

The creek got larger as small streams fed into it, boring deeper and deeper into the landscape until we were soon in a rugged canyon. I realized we were following Deep Creek down off the Flattops.

If Hap succeeded in outrunning this Tracker fellow, we would soon come out in a valley where Deep Creek met the Colorado River. I had driven the road along that valley many times, and there was a Girl Scout camp and dude ranch there, close to the intersection of the two waterways.

I began to think I might be able to bail off and run for help at the ranch, and Hap wouldn't dare follow me, for fear of being shot.

I began to feel a glimmer of hope. My ribs were beginning to get sore from being bounced against his back, and I was eager to end this fiasco. I kept wondering if I was in a dream.

It was hard for me to think about what had happened, it all came about so fast, but how in hell did I end up riding a Bigfoot down off the Flattops—and not only that, carrying what appeared to be a very important book inside my jacket?

The irony and fantasy of it all struck me, and I wondered if I'd somehow fallen into an alternate reality, one far from my own world.

I found out later that I had, but not in the way I imagined. It was a very real world, one based on the same planet I lived on, but one hidden in secrecy and fear—the world of Bigfoot.

And now it was evening, and the sun's rays were at an oblique angle, carrying the glow of sunset on them with a promise of dawn in distant lands. Hap finally stopped, sides heaving, and below us I could see the lights of the Girl Scout camp.

I again felt a great sense of hope, one that would soon be dashed and replaced instead by a great sense of adventure.

CHAPTER 4

"If you go inside and get food, you must return. If Tracker knows the book is inside, he may stop at nothing. Innocent lives are in your hands."

Hap and I stood across the road, hidden in a thicket of willows, watching people come and go into what appeared to be a dining hall. Hap knew I was hungry and wanted to go inside, and he was also well aware of the danger that I wouldn't return.

I wondered if maybe I should give the book to him and be done with it all, go inside, get a ride back to my truck from someone, and forget all this.

It seemed like a dream anyway, and nobody would believe me, so why not just end it and go back to my old life? It would be the sane thing to do. What had I been thinking to steal the Book of Runes?

I was exhausted and hungry and in shock, and I paused for a long time, then unzipped my jacket and took the book out, handing it to Hap.

"I don't want it," he cast, refusing to take it. "They'll kill me. We have to go together now. If you take it inside and stay, Tracker might come inside and kill. He's nearby, waiting, a strong presence. Tracker doesn't want to be close to

14

humans, but will if pushed. But I need you to accomplish this task. We need human resources to hide and travel. Otherwise, we're both dead."

I had no idea what we were supposed to be doing, but Hap seemed to have some kind of plan for the book. But right now, I was starving and needed food, and it was right there through that door. I had no loyalty at all to this big beast—his fate wasn't my concern, my own fate was. I needed to ditch the book and escape.

I quickly slipped away, heading towards one of the nearby cabins. I'd seen a man leave it for the dining hall, and I hoped it was unlocked.

It wasn't, but the window was open, and it was easy to pry off the screen and crawl in. I slipped inside and grabbed a t-shirt with the words "Free Tibet" on it and put it on, as mine was now in tatters—I didn't want to stand out in the dining hall. I was going to go get something to eat, then decide what to do.

I wanted to ditch the book, but it seemed like it had some kind of strange hold on me, and I wondered if I would be able to get rid of it.

I was leaving the cabin when I noticed a pack on a night stand, and I grabbed it, though I felt bad when I found out what was in it. But the money, credit cards, and ID sure came in handy later—though the owner shut down the credit cards. But I wanted that pack for the book, to make it easier to carry.

I stuffed the book down into the pack, then went into the dining hall. I needed to be quick, and there was a long line at the buffet-style cafeteria.

I grabbed a plate and cut in line, excusing myself as I filled it with things that I could put into my pack—roast beef, fruit, carrots—ignoring the looks I was getting from everyone.

I was soon back where Hap waited, where I quickly wolfed down a ham sandwich. I offered Hap a bite, and he shook his head up and down, which I interpreted to mean "great," but found out later that's how Bigfoot signal displeasure.

Hap wanted nothing to do with my food, and after later watching him feast on leaves, berries, and insects, I realized his diet wasn't like mine—he could survive in the wilds just fine, whereas I couldn't.

It was another lesson in humility, especially later, when I tried his patience many times by needing human food while he could just pick out what he wanted from a forest buffet.

"We go now," Hap cast. "Tracker's nearby. His scent is strong."

Fear cloaked my mind, a fear I knew came from Hap. I put the pack on my back, cinching it on tightly, and we both headed through the thick brush down to the river.

We needed water to cover our scent, but we could no longer walk down the creek, as it had now joined the much larger and deeper Colorado River.

I looked longingly at the camp—its cabins and outbuildings—and I wanted so badly to forget the book and turn and go back to my own kind, my own life. How quickly I had changed my mind about everything, I thought.

But it was too late—I'd set something in motion that I couldn't stop.

Just then, just as Hap's big hand grabbed my shoulder, I smelled an acrid black odor. I could feel the tension in his mind, even though he hadn't cast anything to me. I knew

Tracker was nearby, and I had no intention of meeting him.

There, on the bank of the river, in the last glow of day-light, sat several large rafts, all tied to a makeshift dock along the water. I was panicked, as I could hear something large coming through the underbrush behind us.

I quickly untied the first raft and jumped in, wondering if Hap would join me, but to my surprise, he didn't. I re-member thinking this was maybe a good thing, as I wasn't sure the raft would hold his weight, and just then, the current grabbed hold of the boat and began hurtling me downstream at a good clip.

I still had the Book of Runes, but Hap was gone. I won-dered if Tracker would still follow me now, and I somehow knew he would. How could I possibly hold my own against a creature that even Hap was afraid of?

I grabbed onto the oars and steered the boat directly down the middle of the river where the current was swift-est, wondering if I would survive long enough to escape.

And when I turned to look behind me, I knew I was a goner, for there, easily keeping up with the raft, swam a large black beast, its eyes glowing red in the last light of evening.

CHAPTER 5

My first thought was to throw the book into the river and be done with it. I knew Tracker was right behind me, and I had no idea where Hap was, but it didn't matter now, as Tracker wanted me and the book. Hap was now out of the picture and hopefully safe.

I stopped rowing long enough to remove the pack and open it, taking out the book.

And now, a voice filled my thoughts, a voice thick with desperation.

"Don't do it, Sam. Don't throw it out. We have to complete the mission. My people depend on it. Please, Sam..."

How in heck did Hap know my name was Sam? He hadn't called me that before. And where was he?

I turned back again and noted the red eyes were closer, so I picked up the oars and rowed as hard and fast as I could. I was terrified, and the fear motivated me to push myself beyond what I thought I could do.

I think I ruined my adrenal glands the first few days I was with Hap, because I was always terrified. It took awhile to get used to him and the concept of these huge creatures. Actually, I'm not sure I ever did, to be honest.

I was now barreling along with the current and could barely make out the edges of the river, and only because the last remnants of light were reflected from the sky in the water.

I knew I would soon meet the confluence with the Eagle River and things would get more interesting, as the river would become much larger and swifter.

How in the world would I be able to steer a raft down the Colorado River where it tightened and went through Glenwood Canyon with its sheer walls and rapids? I would never live through the rapids at Shoshone Dam.

Maybe this raft thing wasn't such a good idea and I should've just tossed the book and stayed at the Girl Scout camp, Hap be damned.

I went under a bridge, then another and another, barely missing the pilings, and I knew I'd just passed under both lanes of the freeway and the frontage road. Now I was suddenly in a set of rapids—I'd come to the confluence with the Eagle River.

I looked behind me, and the eyes were gone. I was now making really good time in this faster current, but I knew I couldn't keep going in the dark. I was sure to get tangled up in something and crash and probably drown.

The river had made a big turn and was now heading towards Glenwood Canyon at a really good clip. I knew I would soon be at the Bair Ranch bridge, and running into the bridge pilings in the dark was a real concern.

I needed to ditch the raft somehow and continue on foot, but without Tracker knowing. I wondered if I could get out and hike up to the ranch and get help.

I'm not the world's greatest swimmer, so I knew jumping into the water and trying to reach the bank was an iffy proposition, especially without a life jacket and no idea where the bank really was in the dark, plus I would get the book wet and probably ruin it. But I had to do something quick. And at the speed I was going, I didn't have long to hesitate before it would be too late.

I wondered what had become of Hap. Why was this book such a big deal? I remembered what he said about using human resources to hide and travel, to get rid of Tracker, and a thought began to form.

If my plan worked, I'd not only get rid of Tracker, assuming he was still following me, but I would also get rid of Hap, if he was even still around. I had no desire to travel with a Bigfoot—all I wanted was to find a quiet safe place all alone and see if I could figure out what the book had to tell me.

I steered the raft out of the current and to my left, going along the side of the river opposite the freeway, the side the railroad tracks ran on.

I knew a lot of trains used this route, as it was the main line between Denver and Salt Lake City, and if I could somehow hop one, I'd be rid of my unwanted companions. But how to hop a freight when it's moving 60 miles per hour? That could be tricky.

I managed to beach the raft on the river bank and quickly climb out, the pack secured on my back. I then struggled to push the raft back out into the current, nearly losing my footing and falling into the river, and it was soon caught by the current and sailed away.

I climbed up the steep grade to the railroad tracks, where I dragged some large tree limbs onto the rails, then hiked back down the tracks a ways. If my plan worked and the train slowed down when it saw the debris, I wanted to be towards the end of it to make hopping on board easier.

I crawled under some bushes and waited, every little sound leaving me on edge, as I had no idea where Hap and Tracker were.

With any luck, I would soon leave them both far behind.

CHAPTER 6

I was exhausted and had somehow fallen asleep, and the sound of a train blaring right down on me was a rude awakening. The rumble of the huge cars and engines was a quick reality check—it felt like I was right on the tracks.

I heard the squeal of brakes, and I knew my plan had worked, as the train was slowing down. But it wouldn't take long for the engineer to realize they'd simply hit a bit of wood and then speed back up, so I knew I had to act fast, even though I was half asleep.

I jumped up, made sure the pack was firmly on my back, and reached out for the next boxcar that came by, grabbing the hand rail and hoisting myself up—just as I was ripped off my feet.

I had underestimated the speed of the train, and I knew I would soon lose my grip, as there was no way I could hold on. The train was going just too darn fast. My legs felt like lead.

It was only a split second, but I knew then and there I was probably dead. The train was going too fast, and I couldn't hold on much longer—my fingers were slipping.

But just then, something massive pushed up underneath me, throwing me into the empty boxcar. In shock, I rolled away from the door and into the back of the car, then tried to figure out what had happened.

"Great idea, Sam. Tracker's following the raft, swimming down the river. We lost him."

It was Hap. How had he found me?

He had pushed me up into the car, pulling himself up behind me with lightning speed. I felt grateful, and it wouldn't be the last time I was happy to see him, nor would it be the last time I would be amazed at his strength, speed, and agility.

Hap reached out and closed the boxcar door. I yelled out, but it was too late—we were now sealed inside the car, as the door could only be opened from the outside.

Every railroad bum knows to not close the door on a boxcar, but Hap had obviously never hopped a freight. I groaned.

Hap cast, "You OK?"

I answered, "No, and you won't be either when we need to get off this thing." But Hap didn't understand me.

"Time to teach you thoughtcasting," Hap cast.

I simply nodded my head OK, but Hap took this all wrong.

"It's important we communicate. You have to learn."

I remembered that up and down meant no to the Bigfoot, so I just set there, unable to communicate at any level. It was frustrating.

"We'll practice now," Hap cast.

The noise of the boxcar was loud enough we couldn't have had much of a normal conversation, were we able to talk normally. But thoughtcasting didn't use sound waves, and I could understand him perfectly in spite of the noise.

"Sam, focus your mind. Thoughtcasting is focus. Project a thought right into the center of my forehead. Focus on my forehead."

"What if I'm behind you?" I asked silently, trying to project the thought right into Hap's mind.

"No matter...hey! Understood Sam!"

"It's that easy?" I cast.

"Usually it takes awhile to learn."

"Well, I'm used to being alone and talking to myself. Maybe that's why it was so quick."

For the first time, I saw what was a grin come across Hap's face. I knew he was smiling or I would've been terrified, for he pulled back his lips, baring his big square yellowish teeth, teeth that looked like they could easily tear me apart.

Later, I realized they were like my own teeth, mostly molars, not like the canines that true meat-eaters have—but at that time, I was still very much afraid of him.

"You've locked us in here," I cast, nodding towards the big heavy boxcar door.

Hap stood, easily balancing himself as the boxcar swayed, and went to the door, handily wrenching it open. I could hear the sound of the outside lever falling to the rails and hitting against the wheels, then bouncing off the tracks. He then pulled the door back shut.

He cast, "Keep door closed. Tracker can scent us. He's on the river."

"Jeez, you're one strong hombre. But we've probably passed the raft by now," I cast.

"Tracker's a fast strong swimmer—he almost caught you, did you know?"

"I saw someone's eyes, but I didn't know if it was you or him."

"Tracker will kill us both if he catches us."

"Do you think he can run as fast as this train?"

"No, but if he knows we're on it, he'll try to stop it."

"But he has to be ahead of it to do that."

"True."

"I think we're OK for awhile, Hap. By the way, how did you know my name was Sam?"

"You called yourself that—you were talking to yourself when you were in the cave, and you said Sam."

"Then you understand human talk? Why didn't you understand me when I was trying to talk to you?"

"No, I don't understand much, I just know it's a name. Who's Hap?"

"You are. You smile a lot. That's what we call happy—Hap."

Hap bared his teeth, then slipped back down against the boxcar wall and closed his eyes.

"What does Sam mean?" Hap cast.

"I dunno. It's just my name."

"You need a name with meaning, like Hap. You can be Packy because you carry the pack."

He paused, then cast, "Can Packy sense the fear in here?"

It was then that I noticed—there was someone else there, desperately trying to melt into the corner.

CHAPTER 7

I instinctively pushed myself back against the boxcar wall. It was then that I realized what a strong ally I had in Hap, assuming he really was my ally, that is.

If whoever was in there with us tried anything, there would be hell to pay with Hap, who just sat there, looking towards whoever it was, his eyes glowing red in the dark.

"Can you see what or who it is?" I cast, having the first glimmer of how useful this method of communication could be—nobody could hear you talking. I was also learning that Hap had really good night vision—he could see things I couldn't, even in great detail.

"It's a young human male. Scared."

"Can you tell if he's armed?"

"Hap don't know armed," he cast back.

"Does he carry a weapon?"

"A weapon? No, no sticks or rocks."

"Does he have a gun?"

"Hap don't know gun."

"A weapon—a human weapon. It extends the reach so someone can hurt you better. Makes a lot of noise and sends out a bullet, a thing that can enter your body and kill you."

Hap seemed disturbed. "Yes, Hap know gun. We're taught from birth to fear gun. We call gun the death flinger—it flings the little death thing. One of Hap's Greats was killed by one in the Place Where the Sun Lingers."

"The Place Where the Sun Lingers? Where's that?"

"Where the sun shines last. Where we go, take the book."

"Oh man," I said out loud, sighing.

I knew Hap must mean Canada or even Alaska, and I had no intention of going to either place. But the name he had for a gun made me want to laugh.

Now the guy in the corner asked in a loud whisper, "Is that thing real, dude?" I realized later how brave he had been to say anything.

"Hey, it's OK. It's a Bigfoot, a gentle giant."

"So, you really see it too? It's real?"

"Yeah, it's real. I'm Sam and that's Hap. Where you headed?"

I was hoping to get information on where the train was going.

"Marty. Is that thing really real? It has a name? Are you its friend? I'm now gonna bail off this train, if I can get the door open."

"No need to do that. He won't hurt you."

"I'm getting off in Glenwood. I ain't never hoppin' another freight."

I knew the next town, Glenwood Springs, had a rail yard and sidings. I'd gone there myself many times watching the trains when I felt lonely and lost. Glenwood had been my home before I started living in my truck, back when I could afford a little apartment—back before I got to where I hated civilization and fled.

As if on cue, the train began to slow. Hap peeked out the door through the hole where the missing clamp had been and cast, "What's happening?"

"We're stopping. We must be in the rail yard in Glenwood," I cast back.

"I smell Tracker," Hap cast, and the fear was again overwhelming.

"How could he have caught up with us?" I cast.

"Hey, dude, can you open the door?" Marty was standing, ready to get off, wobbling a bit as the train came to a halt.

"Hap, open the door," I cast.

"No. Smell Tracker. He must've somehow got onto the train."

"Hap, this guy wants to leave. Open it for just a moment."

Hap shrugged his shoulders, then pulled the door open just enough for Marty to jump out, then pulled it closed.

It wasn't but a moment until I heard someone yelling, then screaming, and it sounded like Marty. It was terrible, like he was being pulled apart or something.

I wanted to go out and help him, but Hap wouldn't open the door. Then, after a few minutes, I could hear sirens, and they sounded like they were coming right down to the rail yard.

"Human met Tracker," Hap cast.

"Do you think he hurt him?" I cast back.

"Hap don't know. Tracker's mean, so maybe."

I swore under my breath. How in hellsbells did I get myself into this one? Sure enough, the sirens stopped nearby, and I could now hear Marty talking really loud. He was excited, and I was glad to hear his voice, as it meant he was still alive.

But then it dawned on me that Marty might point the police to our boxcar. Tracker must've scared him to death, and he would want the police to believe his story, so why not tell them about us?

"Hap, we have to get out of here now. The police are probably coming."

"Hap don't know police."

"People with death flingers."

I had a hard time saying it, it was such an odd name, though apt.

Hap stood and wrenched the door open before I could even collect myself. I quickly hoisted the pack over my shoulder, making sure the book was still safe.

Hap was quickly out of the boxcar and grabbed me by the waist as I started out the door, just like one would pick up a child.

"Follow Hap," he cast, setting me on the ground, but then apparently changed his mind, as he again picked me up, setting me on his shoulders and ducking behind the boxcar. I could see several police cars with flashing lights nearby.

And there, over behind them, I could see for just a second a pair of glowing red eyes, just as I felt something hit me in the stomach. It hurt so much I almost threw up.

"Run, Hap, run! Tracker's over in the trees behind the police cars. He's afraid to show himself! He did something to me. I'm hurting real bad, Hap, run!"

I doubled over, barely able to hold on, as Hap ran like the wind, straight for the lights of downtown Glenwood Springs.

CHAPTER 8

The intense pain passed fairly quickly, but my stomach was sore for hours. I knew Tracker had done this, but I had no idea how—he hadn't even been near me.

"Where are you going?" I cast to Hap.

"Humans are the only thing that will keep Tracker away. We have to go into human places. Tell Hap where to go so we won't be seen."

I had no idea where to go. A Bigfoot isn't easily hidden, even in the dark, when you're in the middle of a small resort town where people are walking around after dinner enjoying the evening.

But a thought occurred to me.

"Hap, run straight down the tracks."

I knew this would take us to the bridge across the river. Hap ran down the tracks, and as we came to the bridge, I pushed on Hap's head and steered him like a big horse, right to the stairs going up the pedestrian bridge that paralleled the vehicle bridge.

It was now late, but a couple of teenaged boys were skateboarding on the nearby sidewalk, and I could see them fleeing when they saw us, terrified.

We were quickly across the bridge, but not before several cars hit their brakes, and I knew they'd seen us. The town was going to have a few Bigfoot reports tonight.

My plan was to ditch Tracker by hiding our scent, but I wasn't sure if it would work.

"Hap, go this way, over to that big fence."

Hap was soon by the fence surrounding the Glenwood Hot Springs. It was a big pool, and I knew it was closed for the night. I'd spent many pleasant hours soaking in that pool, back in my better and happier days.

We were soon in the warm water, all but our noses poking out. My clothes were full of little air pockets that tried to float in the water. There was no way for Tracker to smell us, given all the minerals we were soaking in.

"Good idea," Hap cast.

"Yeah, if we don't turn into prunes," I answered.

"Hap don't know prunes."

I sighed. It was an impossible task to communicate with someone from not only a different culture, but a whole different species.

I cast, "Seriously, Hap, I don't know how long I can stay in here. It's hot."

"Feels good to Hap," he answered.

After a good half-hour or so, I finally had to crawl out. I lay by the pool, cooling off for awhile, then crawled back in, clothes and all. I noticed the pool smelled a bit musky, in spite of the minerals, and I hoped Tracker couldn't find us.

"Hap, what did Tracker do to me?" I cast.

"It's a way to disable animals. Some Bigfoot, those who eat meat, they use it for hunting. It's like thoughtcasting, except you send a force into the body instead of the mind, a powerful force we call bodycasting."

I recalled having read several Bigfoot encounters where similar things had happened, where people had claimed they'd been slugged in the stomach, yet there was nobody near them. The Bigfoot researchers had said it was infrasound.

Infrasound is sound that's below the threshold of human hearing, which is 20 Hertz. Trains and things with big engines produce infrasound. It's a very real thing, and is even produced by weather events and things like earthquakes and avalanches. But for an animal to produce it— well, I'd been very skeptical, to say the least.

But I researched it a bit and found that whales, elephants, hippos, rhinos, giraffes, and even alligators use infrasound to communicate—sometimes over long distances. Whales could use it to communicate for up to hundreds of miles.

Elephants produce infrasound waves that travel through solid ground and are sensed by other herds using their feet, and humans even have relict sound receptors in their feet, as if we used to be able to sense infrasound ourselves.

But I was still skeptical, as that was for communication—how could an animal make one feel like they'd been hit in the stomach?

The answer was in the actual sound waves produced. If the waves are at a low enough frequency, one can actually feel them. Tigers produce infrasound that makes their prey freeze, and infrasound will also produce feelings of awe and fear.

And all the accounts of people feeling like they were being watched—this could easily be them feeling the infrasound a Bigfoot was producing, trying to scare them. And after feeling it myself, I knew it was real, and I had no defense against it.

I crawled back out of the water, wondering where Tracker was and what our next defense should be. We couldn't stay here in the pool forever.

I suspected we'd be safer traveling during the day and hiding at night—if Bigfoot were nocturnal, this would put Tracker at a disadvantage.

And I still had no idea what was in the Book of Runes nor why I was taking it to this Place Where the Sun Lingers. And I now felt like I'd maybe been setup to do this task and thereby been allowed to steal the book.

Maybe it was a plot to get a human involved, since apparently the safety of the book couldn't be ensured without human help.

I mean, there was no question that Tracker was real and was after us, as the fear I felt from Hap was very real and I'd seen Tracker myself—at least his eyes. But my position in all this wasn't so clear. Someone had allowed me to steal the book, whereas other someones didn't want the book stolen—at least, that was the feeling I was beginning to get.

I just lay there by the pool, my clothes dripping. Just then, I heard a howl come from the rim of the canyon high above, a howl that sounded like a cross between a mountain lion, a gorilla, and an evil spirit.

I grabbed the daypack, which was on the concrete ledge by the pool, and, in spite of the steam rising from the hot springs, I couldn't help but shiver.

CHAPTER 9

Hap and I ended up staying in that darn pool half the night. I kept climbing out and cooling off, but I felt like I was starting to get seriously depleted of electrolytes, as well as getting dehydrated.

I'd gotten out of the pool many times to drink from the nearby fountain, but Hap seemed unbothered by the heat and not once did he drink any water. Of course, it all caught up with him the next day, when he got terribly thirsty.

"Tracker gone," Hap finally said matter of factly.

"Will he come back?"

"Yes. He's still looking for us. He can't figure out where we went. He'll eventually backtrack."

"We have to make a plan," I cast. "We have to start moving by day, not at night. And we need to get out of this dang pool. I'm starting to boil."

"So, Packy will help me get the book back to where it belongs?" Hap cast.

"Do I have a choice?"

"Yes, Packy always has a choice," Hap replied thoughtfully. "But Hap needs Packy's help. Hap can't do it without Packy."

"I've been setup, haven't I?" I asked.

"Hap don't know setup."

"Never mind. Why do you need my help so badly?"

"Hap will explain later, but now we must leave. Where can we go among humans to hide? This was a good idea, but it's over. Hap getting hot."

"I don't know how you lasted this long," I replied. "But I have no idea where to go. Maybe we should hop another train. Where are we taking the book?"

"Hap don't know," he cast in reply.

"How can we return the book when we don't know where it belongs?"

"Maps there, in the book, they have the answer."

"Have you looked at them?" I asked.

"No, Hap not allowed to. The book is sacred."

I moaned out loud. "Holy crap. Not sacred. I don't do sacred."

"What? Hap don't understand. Thoughtcast."

I cast, "I'm not superstitious, Hap."

"Hap don't know superstitious."

"You know, sacred and all that. I'm not superstitious."

"Hap hears you but doesn't understand."

I decided this wasn't the time and place to discuss world views, especially with a Bigfoot.

"Never mind," I replied. "How are we supposed to know where we're going if you can't look at the directions?"

"Hap not sure."

He looked dejected, sweat falling from the thick hair on his large brows.

"Maybe the book's not sacred for a human and I can look," I offered.

Hap pulled back a little, and I could tell he wasn't sure what to do.

"Didn't you say the book came from the Place Where the Sun Lingers?" I asked. "If I knew where that was, it would be a start."

"Yes, it's from there. OK, we go now," Hap cast.

I could tell he'd been thinking while we sat in that darn pool and had a plan. And as I travelled with him through this adventure, I came to appreciate the high level of intelligence these creatures have—but at that time, I was still unsure of anything.

Hap pulled his huge body from the pool, and I swear the water level dropped a few inches, even though it was a big deep pool.

He stood dripping for a bit, then unexpectedly picked me up, putting me on his wet shoulders.

"Where are we going?" I cast, now feeling really unsure. Once again, I had the urge to flee and go into town, forget all this. I was deeply regretting my decision to return to the cave.

"Have to find the Place Where the Sun Lingers," Hap answered. "The days are short there in winter and long in summer."

"It has to be north. Have you ever been there?"

"Yes, long ago when Hap was young. Hap was born there."

"Can you find the way back?"

"I don't know. Has been a long time. We need another train."

I bounced along on his shoulders, the first rays of dawn peeking over the cliffs high above. The Rune Cave wasn't really all that far from where we were, as the crow flies, yet it seemed like another lifetime, another world.

We slipped back over the bridge, this time no one seeing us, as it was early and there was nobody around. Hap then ran swift as the wind for about a half mile, ducking in the brush along the tracks.

He then abruptly stopped and sat me down. We were well hidden, and yet we still needed to hike further down the tracks to where the trains would stop.

"Hap, we need to keep going."

Hap just sat there for a bit, then cast, "Tracker expects us to get on the train. He's waiting somewhere to intercept us. He can smell for a long ways."

This made me pause—I recalled reading about how some predators can smell something dead for up to 60 miles, and I wondered if Bigfoot had that kind of sense of smell. Their flat noses said probably not, as the really keen scenters in the animal world usually had snouts, but who knew?

Tracker certainly seemed to be adept at finding us through our scent. I could understand how he could smell Hap, but I knew he would also be quite capable at tracking me, and I didn't have what seemed to be Bigfoot scent glands.

I was now hungry and pulled off the pack and dug inside where I'd put food from the buffet at the ranch. I pulled out some dried-out roast beef and cheese, then offered Hap some carrots. He took them, a mere sliver of food for someone as huge as he was.

We sat there and munched for a bit, then Hap reached out and started eating the leaves of what looked like some kind of wild berry bush, maybe a serviceberry.

It was then that I remembered the wallet in the pack. I pulled it out and opened it—inside were three credit cards, a driver's license, and about $800 in cash. The picture on the driver's license really didn't look much like me, but I thought I might be able to pass for its owner, Terry Murphy, if someone didn't look too close. A plan began to form in my puny human brain.

"Hap," I cast. "We need to get past where we jumped off the train. That's out in West Glenwood, and one of the car dealers there rents cars. We can rent a car and leave Tracker in the dust."

"Hap don't know car," he replied.

"The things humans ride in that go fast."

"Oh, the moving box? Ride in one?" Hap looked dubious.

"It would have to be a van or an SUV, something that would carry a big guy like you," I cast.

For some reason, I was reminded of the movie, "Harry and the Hendersons." I hoped our trip wouldn't be an escapade like theirs was, if you know what I mean. But then this was real and that was Hollywood, where anything could happen.

Hap lifted me back onto his shoulders and we quickly crept along the tracks back to where the rail yard was. There he paused, hidden in a grove of trees next to the river. I knew he was worried about Tracker.

I cast, "We have to get past the rail yard, then cross back over the river. There's another bridge ahead we can use. But we have to move fast. It's getting light, and someone may see us."

Hap now ran fast, and we were soon at a bridge that crossed the Colorado River, connecting back over to the freeway. We passed a motel and were soon in the shrubs near a car dealership with a small office that said "Glenwood Car Rentals." It was closed.

I had no idea what time it was, nor when they would open, so we crawled back into the bushes and waited. I drifted off to sleep and woke more refreshed, feeling like I'd slept several hours.

Hap was poking me in the ribs, trying to wake me up. The sun was now high in the sky, and I guessed it to be about nine a.m.

I stood and brushed myself off, told Hap to wait, and went into the rental agency.

A young woman with brown hair came to the front desk, asking if she could help me. The largest vehicle they had for rent was a white Ford Econovan, so I took that.

She took the driver's license and copied the number, saying nothing, then, when she'd finished the paperwork, asked for my credit card. I held my breath, hoping it would clear.

It didn't. The owner had obviously called the cards in as stolen, so I just handed her cash, muttering something about how they kept saying my card was stolen when it wasn't and how I was going to cancel the darn thing.

She didn't bat an eye, took me out to the van, unlocked it, showed me how a few things worked, and handed me the keys. It was all too easy, and I've never been able to rent a car before or since without a valid credit card.

I rented it for two days, as I didn't want to use all the cash I had, and I told her my destination was Kansas City, the opposite direction we were going.

Sighing with relief, I pulled out of the drive and headed back to where I'd left Hap in the bushes, then got out and called to him.

I waited for awhile, then walked around looking for him, but with no luck. I thought I smelled his musky odor at one point, but wasn't sure.

Hap was gone and was nowhere to be found. I was free to go wherever I wanted, the Book of Runes be damned.

It was then that I smelled that acrid black odor. Tracker was near!

CHAPTER 10

I wanted nothing more than to toss the book out the window and get out of there, driving as fast and as far as I could to a place where neither Hap nor Tracker nor any of their kind would ever find me.

And I had an inkling of where that place might be—somewhere in the desert, where Bigfoot never went because there was no food nor water.

I grabbed the pack from the seat beside me, then hesitated for just a moment. What if it really were something that Hap's species depended on—what if our taking the book back to the Place Where the Sun Lingers really did matter? I had no idea why it might be, but what if an entire species was depending on me at this very moment?

It didn't make sense—but none of this did. Why did they want to take the book back? Why was it supposedly sacred and why did they need a mere human like me to help?

Too many questions, none that I could answer, and I actually didn't even care at that point. I just wanted to get away from it all.

I mean, I had PTSD—I wasn't the one to do anything daring or courageous, I would just run like a rabbit if put in that position. I couldn't deal with stress, that's why I'd been living in the wilds in my truck.

But that acrid black odor worried me, and I found myself wondering if Hap were OK. I wondered if it were possible to thoughtcast when you couldn't see the one you wanted to cast to.

I sat there by the road next to the bushes, the river just beyond, trying to picture Hap's big coarse face, his heavy brow and deep-set eyes and large lips, that face that was a blend between a gorilla and a human.

And then I cast, "Hap, where are you?"

Nothing, no response.

I tried it again.

"Hap, I'm over here where I left you, waiting. Tracker's near. Hurry, get over here."

I waited—nothing.

I now had an even stronger urge to flee—my intuition was telling me something was seriously wrong. I jammed the van into gear and was ready to tear out when I heard it.

"Packy, come get me. I'm by the bridge. Hurry."

I can't tell you the feeling of relief I had. I spun out and high-tailed it for the bridge.

It was now mid-morning and people were out and about, lots of traffic, but I managed to get over there pretty quick.

I jumped out of the van and ran around to the passenger side and opened the big sliding door.

"Hap, c'mon. I'm here. Get in!"

Just then, I heard a woman scream and saw a car swerve. Hap had been on the other side of the road and was now coming across, terrifying anyone who had the luck to see him. There would be yet more Bigfoot sightings in Glenwood Springs, I suspected.

Hap ran up to the van, ducked his head, and jumped in, the van groaning from the weight. There was no way he could sit in the seat, so he kind of half lay across it, his feet almost preventing me from closing the door, but I managed.

I ran back around and jumped in the driver's side, ignoring the cars that had stopped in disbelief at seeing a Bigfoot get into a van.

And they had plenty more to disbelieve, for just then, a giant beast emerged from the banks of the river, covered with leaves and mud, snarling a snarl that turned into a full-on scream as I gunned the van and tore off. I knew I had narrowly avoided another infrasound episode and felt lucky.

It was truly the biggest and ugliest Bigfoot I'd ever seen. Of course, I'd only seen one other, Hap, who wasn't really all that pretty himself, at least not to me.

Then the beast screamed, and it was so loud I thought it would break my eardrums, but Hap and I were soon long gone, heading west on the freeway, leaving Tracker in the dust.

Or so we hoped, anyway.

CHAPTER 11

I have no idea how many hours it took of hard driving until I felt comfortable enough to stop and take a break. I would occasionally look back at Hap, and he was sound asleep in the back seat, or the part of him that fit on it.

He spilled over on all sides, way too big to be riding in the back seat of a van, but he managed to scrunch himself up. I was amazed that he no longer had that musky smell. It was almost as if he'd somehow turned it off.

When we first took off, Hap covered his big head with his arms and began casting fear to me, a wordless painful kind of fear. It took a long time to convince him that riding in a car was safe, that he would be OK.

He finally settled down, but only after raising his head a number of times, scaring the heck out of whoever happened to be on the freeway at that time and could see him. I finally convinced him to stay down, hidden, and I was glad to see him sleep.

We made good time, rolling on down the freeway past the towns of New Castle, Silt, and Rifle, and I kept looking in the rearview mirror, half expecting to see Tracker.

I was still in shock from the sight of the big ugly beast, and I hoped to never see him again. I was pushing the pedal to the metal the whole time, going over the speed limit a bit, but not enough to get pulled over, cause I sure didn't want a patrolman looking at that stolen ID.

After several hours on I-70, we came to the little desert town of Green River, Utah. I decided to stop for gas and to get something to eat.

I pulled next to the little grocery store there, the Melon Vine, and went inside. I was careful to park kind of around the corner from the parking lot.

I bought stuff for sandwiches, several gallons of Arizona Tea, and a couple of gallon jugs of water, then drove out to the edge of town, where I stopped at a desolate place in the creosote brush so Hap could get out for a bit and stretch his legs without being seen.

Hap got out and looked around, then cast that he was thirsty, so I handed him a gallon of water, and he quickly drank it.

I'd never seen anything like it, whoosh, the water went down his gullet like pouring it down the drain. It was one of many times that I realized how big of an animal he really was.

He now cast that he was still thirsty, so I gave him a gallon jug of tea. I had shown him how to take the lid off the water, so he practiced on the tea with great success, then stood and sniffed it and handed it back.

"Something's wrong," he cast.

"No, try it, you'll like it. It has sugar in it," I replied.

"Hap don't know sugar." He sniffed it again, then tried to stick his big tongue down into the jug. His tongue had a greenish tint to it, which I figured was from eating bushes and shrubs.

He finally tipped the jug up a bit and tasted it, making a face, which was scary, seeing that big hairy forehead all scrunched up—it would be the stuff of nightmares in a different setting.

He then drank the tea down, just like he'd done the water, like pouring it down the drain. It was like he didn't even swallow, just glug glug glug. I had to laugh at how he then smacked his lips.

"Hap still thirsty," he cast, eyeing the other jugs of tea.

"Oh man," I groaned. Feeding and watering a Bigfoot wasn't going to be easy. He drank all the water and tea, and was finally happy again.

"Hap, we have to make a decision now," I cast.

"What?"

"Where are we going? If we want to go north, we have to get off the freeway here. Otherwise, we end up west, eventually in California."

"Hap don't know California."

"A lot of your kind know it. There are Bigfoot out there. But where are we taking the Book of Runes?"

"Hap don't know."

I was frustrated. I didn't worry about Tracker any more, as there was no way he could possibly catch up to us at this point, but I wanted to know where we were going. I had to know, actually, before we could go anywhere.

We sat there for awhile. Hap sampled a bit of creosote brush, then spit it out.

"Are you hungry?" I cast.

"Yes. Need to go to the forest so can find food."

That was the answer I needed. We would turn north and head to the small town of Price, Utah, then on up onto Soldier Summit, up in the forests of the Wasatch Plateau,

where we could find a little side road or something, somewhere Hap could find something to eat and where we
could spend the night.

I was exhausted. It was a feeling that would become my
close companion throughout this long ordeal.

We got back on the road, but I hadn't gone far when
the irony of it all hit me hard, and I kept wanting to turn
around and make sure there really was a Bigfoot on the
back seat of the van.

It seemed the most unlikely thing I could imagine, and
again I felt like I was in a dream, a feeling I would have a
million times over.

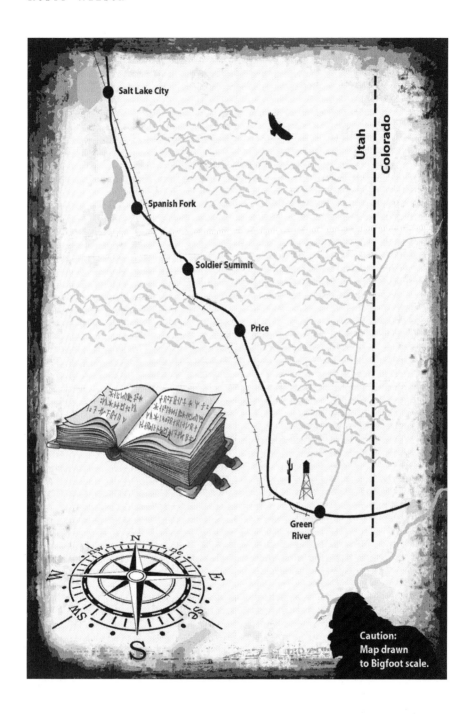

CHAPTER 12

Maybe it actually was a dream, as I have absolutely nothing to prove all this happened, nothing except the photos of the book that the linguistics prof has—and a sketch above my fireplace.

We got to the next town, Price, and the first thing I noticed was a Walmart. I pulled around to the side of the store, told Hap to stay down, hid my pack with the Book of Runes under the seat and went inside.

When I emerged, I had two king sheets, a sleeping bag and pad, some new boots and socks, a few more groceries, and more jugs of water and tea. I'd spent plenty of money, and I knew that I would soon run out if I wasn't more frugal. I needed all I had for gas, as we had a long ways to go.

And I also knew that once we reached the Canadian border, we'd have to ditch the van and go through on foot, as I didn't have a passport and by then the van would probably be listed as stolen.

I had no idea how I could possibly travel by foot and keep up with Hap, and the poor guy couldn't carry me all the time. We'd just have to wait and see how it all went.

We were a good two days from the border, and I only legally had the van until tomorrow—just another thing to consider in all this chaos, but I refused to worry about it.

The worst that could happen is we got pulled over and the state trooper either died of shock upon seeing Hap or tried to shoot him. If he tried to shoot him, I would shoot first with the Glock I carried in my pocket.

Realizing what I'd just thought gave me pause—I would really consider shooting a human to prevent a Bigfoot from being killed?

It was then that I realized I was beginning to feel attached to the big lug, and it hadn't taken very long. And I already knew I didn't think much of most of the human race, so it really was no surprise.

I opened the sheets and draped them over Hap.

"You have to keep these over you," I cast. "We're coming to a large city, and I can't risk anyone seeing you."

"Hap don't know city," he answered.

"Consider yourself lucky. And yes, I know you don't know lucky—it's when things are going good for you."

I was beginning to see a pattern here, but it was one I had to admire. Hap knew almost nothing about humans and their so-called civilization, and I did consider him lucky. I wished I were so lucky.

We got back on the main road and immediately began the climb up Soldier Summit, a pass that eventually dropped into the big wide valley that held the Great Salt Lake and the city named for it. As we drove on, the highway went up a canyon with railroad tracks on the other side.

As we climbed up the grade, we soon left the desert and entered a high grasslands and forest. I noted the shadows were getting long and decided it would be a good idea to stop on top and find a place to camp for the night.

Hap was now snoring, and the sound pretty much rocked the van, it was so loud. I was now pretty sure that Bigfoot was a nocturnal animal, which would make sense, given that humans were probably their main enemy. Bigfoot would be smart to forage for food by night when people slept.

We were now on top of the pass, and I saw a dirt road take off on my left. It climbed up in big sweeping curves, going to a subdivision of exclusive mountain homes, according to the big real estate sign by the road.

It didn't look like anyone was rushing to buy the land and build on it, as I could see only one log house high above in the aspens.

I pulled off the main highway, then noticed another road that took off and climbed a small hill to what looked to be some kind of microwave tower, so I turned onto that.

We climbed a bit and were soon parked next to the fence surrounding the tower. This looked like a good spot to spend the night—it was very unlikely anyone would come up here.

I turned the van around, a habit I've had for years in case I needed to make a quick exit, then cut the engine. Hap still slept, so I got out and found a good spot for my sleeping bag and began blowing up the pad, then spread the bag out.

It was almost dark, and I was hungry, so I made myself some PBJ sandwiches and sat on the van bumper and ate while Hap snored away.

I could hear a train in the distance, coming up the grade we'd just climbed from Price. I had finished my sandwiches by the time the train made it to the top of the grade, just below us, so I walked over to the edge to get a better look. It was just below me when it sounded the whistle for the road crossing. I thought this was cool, as I love train whistles, but I hadn't predicted Hap's reaction.

He came flying out of the van in a panic.

"Packy! Packy!"

"Over here," I answered.

"Packy! What is it?"

Hap was now by my side, and upon seeing the train below, he relaxed.

"Were you having a bad dream?" I cast.

"Yes. Tracker's still looking for us."

"We're so far ahead of him he could never catch up."

"Never underestimate Tracker."

"Never underestimate pure evil," I replied, then added, "I know, you don't know evil. But you know Tracker. He's evil, so you do know evil, I guess."

Hap was surveying the countryside around us. He soon cast, "Hap hungry. Up above here, there's food. Be back later."

"OK, Hap, but I'll be sleeping. You really don't think Tracker could be nearby, do you? I hope he wasn't somehow on that train."

Without answering, Hap was gone in the blink of an eye, up into the aspen forest above us towards where that lone house set. Now that it was dark, I could see it had lights shining inside—someone was home.

I hoped Hap would stay far away from it, as people in these parts were typically well-armed. The state of Utah had practically invented target practice, as far as I knew.

I settled into my sleeping bag, weary. Venus was exceptionally bright, hanging right at the handle of the Pleiades in the western sky. I watched a satellite track high above, and then quickly was asleep.

It didn't seem like I'd been asleep but a few minutes when I was awakened by a gunshot, followed by a shrieking howl that made my blood curdle.

I managed to get out of my bag and into the van, locking the doors, just as two glowing red eyes came into view. I was still mostly asleep, and all I could figure was that Tracker had found us.

CHAPTER 13

Hap was now casting to me, "But they had food, right there in the maybe-food thing by the people box, and Hap smelled round-yums. Hap couldn't help himself."

Fortunately, it was Hap's eyes I'd seen, and he was alright, although I guessed the people who had shot at him were probably packing their stuff to leave after hearing him howl.

"What in heck's a 'maybe-food thing,' and what's a 'round-yum'?" I asked, frustrated. All I needed was a wounded Bigfoot on my hands—I had enough going on already.

As Hap was casting it again, I realized he was talking about a trashcan with left-over pancakes. I had to laugh.

"You risked your life for pancakes—excuse me, round-yums? Did you manage to find any?"

Hap looked upset. "No."

"Still hungry?"

"Yes."

"Hap, I could easily have got you pancakes if I'd known. We'll get some tomorrow. Can't you go find some leaves or something to eat for now?"

"Not as good as round-yums," Hap answered dejectedly.

"Well, I need some sleep. Tomorrow we'll get you pancakes. But stay away from that house, Hap."

"No worries. Pan-cake. Why?"

"A cake made in a pan. Do you know cake?"

"Yes."

This surprised me, but I later found out that Hap knew more than I had at first guessed, but mostly about edible stuff. He apparently had hung around human houses enough to know what was good eating. I bet the owners of the trashcans that had cured his midnight hunger had no idea.

I crawled back into my sleeping bag and was soon asleep again, not waking until dawn. I then noticed a big lump nearby that hadn't been there before.

Next to me slept a big hairy Bigfoot, and it didn't scare me one bit, in fact, it made me feel more secure, knowing this big guy was becoming my friend and would look out for me.

I had to shake my head at the knowledge that I was no longer afraid of Hap, but that's how it is—the more you know, the less you fear.

I slipped out of my bag just as the sun rose over the trees on the hillside across from us. Another train was coming, and as it clickity clacked up the tracks below us, I ate a granola bar and tried to wake up. I really wanted some coffee, but no luck on that front.

I finally had to wake Hap up so we could get going. I nudged him a bit with my toe while casting for him to get up.

He rolled over and yawned, then stretched, and his big muscles rippled under his dark skin.

"What now, Hap?" I cast.

"Pancakes," he replied, grinning his wide grin, his yellow teeth showing.

"OK, let's get going. We'll get you some pancakes."

Hap scrunched back into the van and I placed the sheets over him, then got in and started up. We would soon be in the Salt Lake metro area, and I was having serious second thoughts about trying to drive through a city with a Bigfoot in the back.

Too many things could go wrong—a flat tire, getting pulled over by the cops, someone seeing Hap, just too many things for me to feel comfortable.

But as they say, the quickest way out is through, so I headed for Salt Lake, as it seemed to be the fastest way north. We had a limited amount of time with the van, and we needed to get as far north as possible before our ride ended. We would just have to take our chances.

As we came out of Spanish Fork Canyon, which opens into the Great Salt Lake Valley, I once again felt Hap communicating fear to me.

"What's up, Hap?" I cast.

He cast nothing back but more fear, but I soon saw the source of his worries—ahead of us was a wind farm, its huge wind turbines turning in the steady breeze.

"It's OK, Hap," I cast. "It's just a wind farm."

"Hap don't know wind farm," he replied.

"Big machines that make electricity from the wind."

I knew it was hopeless. Hap wouldn't know wind, machine, or electricity. But I was wrong, he cast back that he knew wind, though he had no idea what caused it. But what was electricity?

"You know, like in the house last night, light." I pointed at the sun. "These big things catch the wind and make it into light so people can see at night. You're lucky, you don't need night light, you see just fine, but humans don't. Now stay hidden, we're in the city."

Hap ducked back down and pulled the sheet over his head. I hoped he would go back to sleep, which he apparently did, as we had no mishaps for the couple of hours it took to negotiate the freeway through Salt Lake City, and I didn't hear a peep out of him.

After some time, the city seemed to gradually be falling behind us, and I knew we had to soon stop for gas and food. I had stopped once at a pleasant little deli in Brigham City, and that was where I wanted to go again. It wouldn't be long before we were crossing the highlands that separated Utah from Idaho, and there weren't many places to stop.

I took the Brigham City exit and found a gas station, filling the tank. That dang van got really poor mileage, and at that rate, we would soon be walking, as my money was quickly disappearing.

I drove on over to the deli and parked, once again halfway around the back.

Before Hap could raise his ugly head, I cast, "Hap, stay down. I'm getting pancakes. Be right back."

Hap answered with what sounded like a little kid giggling, a little kid with a big giggle.

By the front door was a rack with day-old baked goods, and I grabbed a half-dozen or so packages of cinnamon rolls. Hap would love these, I figured. I then got myself a tuna sandwich and some potato soup to go and went back to the van.

I handed Hap a package of rolls, then sat there and ate my lunch. I could hear him happily munching, then a big black hairy hand reached up and grabbed the sack with the rest of the rolls.

"Don't make yourself sick, Hap," I cast. "That's a lot of rolls."

"A small snack for a Bigfoot," Hap answered happily. He soon tossed the sack back into the front, empty except for plastic wrapping.

"More," he demanded.

"Seriously?"

"Please, Packy. Hap hungry. More."

I shook my head, then dutifully went back inside, where I bought everything on the rack—more cinnamon rolls, jalapeño cheese bread, chocolate cupcakes, raspberry rolls, pumpkin spice bread, cream-cheese rolls, well, you get the drift.

It was a pretty good-sized bakery and had lots of stuff. I had to make two trips to get it all, and the counter help seemed a bit surprised—until I mumbled something about it being for a Bigfoot, and then they laughed.

I put everything on the seat, admonished Hap not to eat it all at once, then headed back onto the freeway, helping myself to a piece of chocolate-swirl cake.

I felt a strange sense of well-being—something about being so well-stocked with sugary baked goods, maybe—and it surprised me, given the circumstances. I had no idea where we were going, I had thrown my lot in with a mythical creature, and we had a killer on our trail, hardly the stuff to make one feel happy.

But it was a feeling destined to end soon. We hadn't been on the freeway more than 20 minutes when I looked back and saw a Utah state trooper coming up behind me, his lights flashing and siren on.

I hoped he was after someone else, but I knew he wasn't when he got right on my tail and followed directly behind me, signaling for me to stop.

One of my worst fears was about to come true.

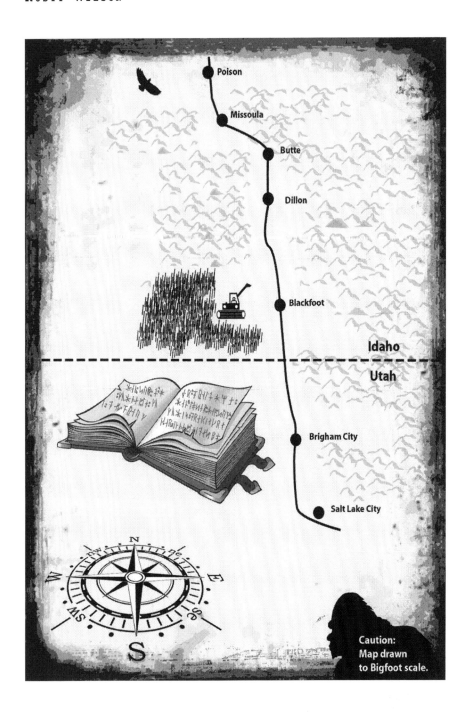

Poison

Missoula

Butte

Dillon

Blackfoot

Idaho

Utah

Brigham City

Salt Lake City

Caution:
Map drawn
to Bigfoot scale.

CHAPTER 14

My feeling of well-being had quickly become one of desperation as I pulled onto the edge of the freeway. I had a stolen driver's license, and it would be the first thing the trooper would check out.

I would then be arrested, and then either taken to jail or Hap would come to my defense. I would be obliged to shoot if the trooper pulled his gun, and I could see things would quickly disintegrate into violence and a possible manhunt.

"Why are we stopping?" Hap asked.

"Hap, stay down. Police. Death flingers. No matter what, stay down."

Hap grunted, and I knew he was still munching away on baked goods. The pile on the seat had seriously diminished.

I had to think fast. The trooper was taking his time getting out of the car, probably running the plates, I figured. They probably wouldn't be listed as stolen yet, but when he saw my fake ID, I knew I would be history.

I grabbed a pen from my pocket and tore one of the bakery sacks in half and started writing on it.

By the time the trooper had come to my window, I was done, and I handed him the note. He seemed surprised and suspicious, but read it, then stood there for a moment as if not sure what to do or say.

Of course, just then Hap had to lift his head up, in spite of my warning to stay down. I knew what was happening from the look on the trooper's face.

As Hap slowly raised his head, the guy's eyes followed him, and the expression on his face turned to shock and horror.

He turned white as a sheet, then quickly got into his police car. Just then, Hap opened the van window and heaved up everything he'd eaten onto the pavement.

I was a bit miffed at Hap for ignoring me, but his appearance was at least timely. Besides, he hadn't thrown up in the van, which was good.

But now what? There was no way I could outrun a state trooper in a van, and he was just sitting there.

"What did Packy do?" Hap cast.

"I wrote him a note, and I know, you don't know note. It's a way for humans to communicate without talking, like thoughtcasting, but we write stuff on paper. Like the Book of Runes, thoughts on paper."

"What did Packy write?"

"I wrote something like this: Not a joke. Bigfoot in back. Don't shoot."

Hap seemed pleased with himself when he answered. "Packy, Hap did good, showing his face. Don't be mad. Hap couldn't help it."

"I know, Hap, I know. But now what do we do?"

"Will he use the death flinger? No one captures Packy or Hap."

"I don't know. Stay down. Nobody's going to capture you, Hap, not if I can help it, anyway."

I finally decided to pull back onto the freeway. The trooper just sat there, and I suspected he had decided to give it all up, that it wasn't worth the hassle and humiliation of having to tell anyone what he'd seen. Nobody would believe him, and he might even lose his job. He was probably in shock.

Hap and me, we'd gotten real lucky that time. If we'd had to abandon ship, we would've had a lot further to hike, and as it turned out, it would be plenty far enough.

We finally reached Pocatello, Idaho, where I had to stop once again for gas. I counted my money—not much left. I got more coffee and some cheese nachos, the kind where you squirt this fake plastic cheese over some chips in a little dish.

When I got back into the van, Hap was still under the sheets, but I knew he was awake because he cast about the nachos. He liked the smell and wanted some, so I went back in and got several more orders for him.

Man, I now figured his blossoming junk-food diet was going to kill him off before we could get to Canada or wherever it was we were going.

I pulled back onto the freeway, still headed north, and we soon reached the small town of Blackfoot.

It would soon be dark, and we needed to stop. We were surrounded by large fields, a kind of rolling landscape with distant horizons. I took the next exit, which didn't appear to go much of anywhere—a farm exit—and headed east.

I soon found a narrow dirt road that wound into a huge wheat field. I pulled onto it, winding back down along a small draw, stopping where I knew we couldn't be seen from the road.

The draw was filled with murky green water and lots of cattails, and I figured it would be mosquito land, and I was right, they were thick.

But I didn't get bit once, and I was later to realize that Hap's natural musky odor was a great mosquito deterrent. If he were in the area, the mosquitoes would flee, just like about everything else. As soon as he got out of the van, the clouds of mosquitoes were gone.

I found a nice soft spot to lay out my sleeping bag and pad, then kicked back and relaxed a little. Hap had quickly gone to work on the cattails, devouring them with gusto. He was hungry, and apparently they were pretty tasty.

It was now evening, and the temperature was perfect for sleeping. Crickets were chirping, and off in the distance, I could hear some kind of owl calling.

I wondered why sometimes everything was silent around Hap, and other times not. I'd read many accounts where everything became deathly silent when a Bigfoot was near, but so far that hadn't entirely been the case with Hap.

Hap had gone up onto a small nearby ridge to scope out the countryside, and I'd just crawled into my bag when a thought came almost blasting into my mind.

"Packy, there's something coming this way. I can see it out in the fields. It's big and it's black and it's moving fast."

It was Hap, casting to me from up on the ridge, a message that made my blood run cold, in spite of the warm balmy evening.

CHAPTER 15

I was up as fast as I could, headed for the van. I threw my bag and pad into the back, jumped in, and started the engine.

"C'mon, Hap, let's go," I cast frantically.

He was still up on the ridge, watching the figure get nearer, its blackness contrasting with the yellow dryland wheat stubble in what was left of the evening light.

Hap hadn't yet come down, and I was getting more and more nervous. It had to be Tracker. What else would be out in these huge fields of wheat? How could he have possibly caught up to us?

Anything to do with Tracker was beginning to have a strange almost supernatural feel to it, and yet I knew he was just another Bigfoot, flesh and blood like Hap, for I'd seen him myself.

Now Hap cast to me, "It's almost here, Packy. Hap come down now. Time to go."

Before I could snap my fingers, Hap was in the van. I spun out, catching the back wheelwell on a small tree stump. The van just sat there, spinning out, the stump big enough to stop us.

Just as I was ready to ask Hap to get out and lift the van off, a huge black head appeared at the edge of the field above the draw. It was black as tar and looked down at us ominously. I felt half sick, knowing it was Tracker.

But in the evening light, as it stood there, looking down on us, I could then see it had two horns, and the hair on its face was curly. It had large nostrils, and I could hear it snorting.

It was a bull—a big black Angus bull. A free-ranging and curious bull that had come to see what was in its territory.

Now Hap got out, stood full height, and made a soft bellow. I had expected him to scare the bull off, but instead he seemed to be talking to it.

The bull stood there for a moment, snorted, then turned and casually walked back down the road, heading back to where it came from.

Hap turned and lifted the van free. I got out and stood there for awhile, then cast, "Will it come back?"

"No," Hap replied. "It just wanted to see what was going on."

"Did you talk to it?"

"In a fashion. Not like we talk, but it understood we meant no harm. Packy sleep in peace."

I took my bag back out of the van, then reconsidered. I would sleep in the van tonight.

"Packy frightened?" Hap asked.

"No. Well, maybe a little. The thought of Tracker being around isn't very pleasant."

"Don't worry. Hap be up all night, watching."

"Thanks, Hap."

"It's OK. Hap always stays up all night. Hap a Bigfoot."

I went and sat down on a large nearby rock. Hap leaned against the van, and I could see it tip a bit. The stars had now come out as the last evening light faded, and I could make out the Big Dipper, Taurus, the Pleiades, and a few other constellations.

The night suddenly seemed overwhelming. It was an old feeling, one I'd had many times before, and I wished I could build a fire, as that seemed to be the only thing that would bring me warmth at such times—not just physical warmth, but mental and emotional warmth.

"Hap, I've known you for only two days, but it feels like we're friends. Do you know friends?"

"Yes, Packy, Hap know friends."

"How can it be that we're now friends so quickly?"

"Hap and Packy share a common goal—and enemy."

"Well, I dunno, maybe that's a bit of a stretch. I'm not so sure I care that much about taking the Book of Runes to Canada or wherever we're going. Where the heck are we going, Hap?"

"Hap don't know."

Right then and there I decided to open the book in the early morning when Hap would still be sleeping and look at the maps. I couldn't take this any longer, I had to know. It was my life, my future, too.

I then immediately felt guilty and wondered if Hap could tell what I was thinking.

The evening stretched out before us like the wheat field we sat next to, and a strange sense of melancholy overtook me.

"Hap, when I was a kid, I used to go stay on my uncle's wheat farm in Nebraska. I know that means nothing to you, but it makes me feel lonely now, sitting here. It was a long time ago. Do you ever feel lonely, Hap? Hap know lonely?"

"Hap do, Packy. Hap know lonely."

"Sometimes I wish I had a home. Do you know home, or are you and your kind totally nomadic?"

"Hap once long ago know home, Packy."

"Sometimes, Hap, I want to go home so bad it makes me hurt inside. Especially when I realize I have no home."

"Why no home?"

"It takes money to have a house. I don't have any money. And even at that, having a house doesn't really make it home so much, it's people who care about you that makes it a home. There's nobody who cares about me, Hap. I'm not trying to get your sympathy, it's just how it is."

I continued, even though I wasn't sure Hap understood what I was talking about.

"And back when I used to have a home, sometimes the wandering urge would hit me hard, and I'd have to leave. I could hear other places calling to me, lonely places, places like this wheat field in the moonlight here in Idaho, a long ways from home. I'd have to go, because that felt like home, those far away places."

I paused, then continued, "My wife, Amy, she never understood and eventually divorced me, although partially because of my PTSD. There was nothing I could do but follow the feeling, Hap, even though it tore me apart, tore my life apart—still does, actually."

"Hap sorry, Packy. It hurts."

"Yeah, it hurts. Where is your home, Hap?"

"Not sure any more. Bigfoot mate for life, and Hap don't have a mate. Maybe I'll find a home and a mate where we take the Book of Runes. The Greats were from there, my kin. They're dead now."

"Hap, why are we taking the book and where are we going?"

"Hap tell you later. It takes too long. Hap needs more food tonight."

"C'mon, Hap. If I'm going to be your partner in crime, I need to know more."

"Hap don't know partner in crime," he replied. "The book has guided my people for many years, but it's also been disruptive to us. It has to go back to its origins."

"I thought the book was the story of your people, your lore."

"We have no lore. We have no need for lore, we are simple and live for today. It was a book of your lore, what your people taught us. At first, it made our lives better, but then worse."

Hap stopped and listened for a minute, then continued, "Many things were disruptive to Bigfoot, like the rule saying you can't mate with who you love, but must mate by color. Now some little Bigfoot aren't as healthy. And it says Bigfoot have to range, can't stay in one place. Makes finding mate and raising little ones hard, hard to find a home."

I wondered if the mating sanction was resulting in a smaller gene pool and thus inbreeding. If so, this was bad, and the Bigfoot Nation would eventually become sick and die off.

"Hap, why not just throw the book in the trash? Why did I have to get involved?"

Hap cast back, "Because it's a great book, and my kind have to see it end in a great ritual in order to understand. It's deep inside them. It was brought to us by a human and must be destroyed by a human, or they won't believe."

Now Hap turned and walked back up the ridge, quickly disappearing.

I crawled into the van, laying out my sleeping bag on the back seat, and thought about what he'd said. It was the most he'd spoken about the book since we'd met.

Tomorrow, I would open that damn book and figure out for myself what was going on. I would look at the maps. As the driver, I had no choice. I had to know our destination. How the hell else could we possibly get there?

I patted the pack containing the book, making sure it was still under the seat, then promptly fell asleep, dreaming of a huge snowfield with a black figure hiking down it, a figure who looked like Hap and who suddenly fell and disappeared into a deep crevasse.

CHAPTER 16

It was early when I woke, and I felt cramped from sleeping on the seat. I preferred the ground, where I could stretch out, but fear does odd things to one, making me want the safety of the van.

I had tossed and turned all night, Tracker on my mind, as well as the uncertainty of where we were going.

The sun hadn't yet come up, and I could see Hap over by the edge of the field, curled up in a giant ball, sleeping. I was tired of wondering what was going on, and now was my chance to try to make sense of things.

I reached under the seat and retrieved my pack, slowly pulling out the Book of Runes, then checking again to see if Hap was still asleep. He was, so I relaxed a bit, placing the large book on my lap, then slowly and carefully turning the thick pages.

I had no idea what any of it said, as the runes were as Greek to me as real Greek would be. I carefully flipped through the pages, coming to the drawings of the two Bigfoot. They looked almost regal with their crowns, if a Bigfoot could ever look regal with their heavy brows, thick cheeks, and deep set eyes.

I paused, comparing the two to Hap, and the resemblance seemed to be more than just that between members of the same species. For some reason, I got the feeling that these two were Hap's ancestors somehow, maybe his grandparents. It was the eyes and lips—his matched theirs perfectly.

Was Hap somehow of some royal lineage? The thought of such beasts having royalty somehow seemed amusing, and yet not. The thought of humans having royalty would probably be equally amusing to Bigfoot, if they knew.

To me, the thought of any kind of royalty went against the grain. I preferred to think we were all equal, none of us any more special than anyone else.

I'd never thought very highly of social status, and royalty just reeked of one group convincing others they were more special and then using that to exploit them, often using the so-called sacred to brainwash them. Just like sacred, I didn't do royal.

I flipped through the pages of the book, totally intrigued, even though I had no idea what any of it said. The penmanship was beautiful, like that of an artist, like well-done calligraphy. Each rune was a work of art in itself. It must have taken a long time to write the book, I thought, holding the pages by their edges and being very careful to not get any fingerprints or oil on them.

Now I'd come to the end of the book and to the maps. There were three of them, and they were drawn on a different type of paper, very thin and fragile, almost transparent. I sat and studied them for a long time, but nothing made sense. There were mountains and what looked like trails, but nothing to really place it in any context.

I was getting more and more frustrated. I had now defied Hap by looking at the book, and yet it made no difference at all. I still had no idea where we were going or why. The maps made no sense. My role in all this made no sense. Nothing made any sense.

I closed the book just as a huge head filled the window next to me. It was Hap. He'd woken up. Had he seen me reading the book? What would he do?

Fear hit me like a ton of bricks. I instantly realized I was no more his friend than the man in the moon. I was just a medium to get this book wherever they wanted it—Hap and whoever was behind him.

He was huge and could snap my neck like a matchstick. My only hope was that he needed my help more than he valued the sacredness of the book and would thereby let me live.

Hap opened the door and stood there, and I could tell he was very angry—in fact, he was so disturbed he seemed to have trouble thoughtcasting. He finally got it out, and what he cast made me feel sick.

"You have violated the sacred, and now you will die."

CHAPTER 17

I shrugged, not sure what to say or do—and with that, I felt completely relaxed and unafraid. The worst that could happen was for Hap to kill me, and I really didn't even care at that point. I had nothing to lose.

I opened the book back up, ignoring Hap, and turned again to the maps.

"Look, Hap," I cast. "Here are the maps. I've studied them and studied them, and I can't make any sense of anything. See if you can." I handed him the book.

To my surprise, he took it, though reluctantly. He looked like he expected a lightning bolt to come out of the sky, but he took it.

"Let's go over there and sit down," I cast, motioning towards a nearby rock. Hap sat on it, and I sat next to him. Apparently he wasn't going to kill me after all, or maybe he was saving it for later. But I just didn't care.

We sat there, studying the maps, and I could tell Hap was as baffled as I was.

"Does anything look familiar to you?" I asked.

"No."

"Is it the Place Where the Sun Lingers?"

"Hap has no idea."

Now Hap was slowly and very carefully looking through the book. He seemed no longer afraid of it. When he came to the drawings of the two Bigfoot, he stopped. He sat there looking at them for a long time.

"Are they someone you know, Hap?"

"Yes," he replied. "My Great Great Parents."

"No way! Were they special or something?"

"They were the ones who met Erik the Red, who made the book. Hap's Great Great Mother made the paper and cover and put it all together, just like the Red taught her, but Erik the Red wrote the runes."

"Could they read the runes?"

"Hap don't know."

"Who's Erik the Red?"

"He's a sacred being, though human, the one sent to teach Bigfoot how to live."

"Erik the Red sounds like a bloody Viking to me."

"Hap don't know bloody Viking."

"How long ago was this?" I asked.

"Well over 2000 moons," Hap cast in return.

I cast, "Let's see, if a year has approximately 12 moons, that's over 200 years, a long time ago."

"Yes, too long. The book is bringing Bigfoot to ruin."

"The runes are ruining you," I tried to joke, then immediately regretted it. "Hap, are you having to destroy the book because you're their descendant?"

"Yes. It's Hap's burden because I'm Hap."

"That kind of stinks, doesn't it?" I asked. "You're innocent and had nothing to do with it."

"True, but it's also an honor to know they think Hap is capable."

"Who is this they, and why do you care what they think?"

"The elders of the Bigfoot Nation. They've guarded the book for many generations. Then Tracker showed them what the book was doing to Bigfoot. Tracker convinced the elders to have the book returned and destroyed."

"Tracker? Our buddy Tracker? How is he involved in all this?"

"Tracker was once a respected tribal leader, such that Bigfoot follows leaders. Most Bigfoot just lead themselves and aren't followers, but Tracker was influential over many. He saw the damage from being rangers, and said it's not good."

"Rangers?"

"Yes. Bigfoot has to range. Go all over, many many miles. Some prefer home, but they still must range. The book says so."

"So why is Tracker now trying to prevent the very thing he wanted by trying to kill us and get the book?"

"Hap don't know."

"Was Tracker always a killer?"

"Hap don't know. He didn't seem to be, but who knows what's deep in Tracker's heart?"

"What happened to him?"

"Hap don't know."

I leaned back on the rock and closed my eyes, opening them again when Hap handed me the book.

"Here, put it away now," he cast.

"Are you going to kill me?"

Hap looked shocked. "Kill you?"

"Yeah, you said I was going to die because I looked at the sacred book. Look, Hap, it's just a book. I don't know what it says, but the only thing sacred about it is in your head. It's just paper and some chewed hide and ink."

"Bigfoot are taught we will die if we ever touch the book without the sacred ritual first. Hap not threatening to kill Packy, was just telling Packy what would happen."

"Well, we're both still kicking, looks to me. Maybe we're going to die soon, who knows, but if so, it won't be because we looked at some paper with ink on it."

I paused, studying Hap's face. He seemed conflicted.

"Look, Hap, if anything's sacred, it's the ground beneath our feet, this planet. It sure as hell wasn't created by no human or Bigfoot. It's what gives us life, nurtures us, and where we'll go when we die, right back into dust. To me, that's more sacred than some book full of mystical crap."

To my surprise, Hap grinned. It was like he'd never considered what he'd been taught, never even looked at it before this, but now liked the idea of being free from it all. Maybe he was a closet rebel, I thought.

I stuffed the book back into the pack, wishing I could be free of it all myself, then put it back under the seat.

Hap got into the back and pulled the sheets over his head. I knew he would soon be fast asleep, leaving me to my thoughts as I drove along.

We headed out, on our way to a place we weren't even sure existed.

CHAPTER 18

We were soon back on the freeway, where I very carefully watched my speed. More than once an Idaho state trooper passed me, and I was getting paranoid at the police presence I was seeing.

The van was, as of last evening, illegal. My return time was five p.m., and I wondered how long it would take for the rental company to list it as stolen. I figured we had today, and that was about it, that's how long it would take for things to hit the grapevine.

We soon reached Idaho Falls, where I stopped yet again for gas and coffee. I was keeping the tank topped off as best I could in case we had to take a back road, which was very possible if Hap were to somehow cause a stir.

Back on the freeway, we left Idaho and were soon in the long grassy valleys that made up southern Montana. Big mountains flanked us as we drove further north, heading for the town of Dillon.

We would eventually head for Missoula, then on to Kalispell and the Canadian border. Or so I hoped. We still had a long ways to go and very little money. I was getting seriously worried.

We were still on I-15, making good time north, and the state trooper presence seemed to pretty much end when we crossed the Montana state line.

I was able to relax a bit, and we soon reached the small town of Dillon, where I stopped and gassed up yet again, then stopped at an old bus that had been converted to a Mexican food stand. I ordered takeout, and we were soon on the road again, Hap sleeping like a log, which suited me just fine.

This part of Montana seemed pretty isolated, and there wasn't much traffic at all. After driving awhile, I took the exit at the tiny town of Melrose, as I needed to make a pit stop, but instead of turning towards the town, I went to my right onto what looked like a ranch road.

I was soon at a sign that said "Melrose Cemetery," so I turned and went up a small hill. There, on top, was indeed a cemetery, though it looked very old and somewhat abandoned. It looked like a good place to take a quick break.

I got out and walked around a bit looking at the old headstones. Some of the lives recorded were long, others pretty short. I stood there and wondered what it would've been like to live here a hundred years ago, trying to eke out a living as a rancher in such a remote and barren place.

I was startled to hear Hap's voice in my mind, as I'd thought he was asleep.

"Where are we?" he cast.

"It's a cemetery, Hap. Where we put our dead."

"A cemetery? Where are the dead? Hap don't see anyone. What are the stones for?" Hap was now out of the van.

"We put the dead in the ground. Under there." I pointed at a grave. "And the stones have writing, like in the Book of Runes, that tells who is beneath."

Hap said nothing, but I sensed he was puzzled and maybe even a bit disturbed. Finally, he cast, "Why?"

"I don't know," I answered. "That's just how some humans do it, though some prefer to be burned in the fire."

I was beginning to be uncomfortable and could see why he felt that way, too. If he'd taken me to a Bigfoot graveyard, I would probably feel weird, too.

"How do you do it?" I cast to Hap.

Hap answered, "Packy mean, after the Bigfoot dead, what happens?"

"Yeah," I cast. "Nobody's ever found a Bigfoot body. What happens to them?"

"Bigfoot is made so that after we die, we go quickly."

"What does that mean? Where do you go?"

"Bigfoot bodies are different from yours. When Bigfoot die, they are soon nothing. Bigfoot bodies decay very quickly."

"How can that be when you're animals like everything else? Bears and deer and such don't decay quickly like that. You're made of the same types of molecules and atoms as they are, as we all are, you have to be." I was frustrated and perplexed.

"Hap don't know molecules and atoms," he replied.

"Look," I cast. "You're the same as me."

I touched Hap, put my hand on his giant arm, then quickly recoiled, as no, he wasn't like me at all, he felt different. Even though I'd ridden his shoulders, I'd been too sidetracked to notice, but now, here where I could think about it, I could tell he was indeed different.

Not only was he very hot to the touch, he felt like there wasn't much there, like I could almost put my hand through him. It was hard to explain, and it seemed contradictory, that something so large could be so ethereal.

I was shocked. How could this giant beast be different from all other creatures on Earth? I reached out and touched him again, this time holding onto him for a bit. Hap had no idea what I was doing, but he just smiled that toothy grin that had at first terrified me.

He was indeed there, real, but he still felt different. Could he be made of a different chemical or molecular structure from most animals on Earth?

It didn't make sense, as he was a mammal, at least I assumed he was, and we mammals had all evolved basically from the same stuff. Even non-mammals didn't feel like that, they were solid and had the same basic structure as everything else on the planet.

But if Bigfoot were different in some fundamental way, it would explain a lot of things—like the fact a body had never been found, nor a Bigfoot fossil, nor even a single tooth. It would also explain how sometimes they seemed to shimmer and disappear, and how they were able to scale things so quickly and easily.

Could they have possibly taken an evolutionary turn the rest of us had missed? Or were they even related to us at all?

To be honest, I was completely blown away by this and later tried hard to understand how it could work scientifically, but I never did find an answer.

Hap now took my hand from his arm and held onto it for a bit, engulfing it in his big palm.

"Very cold," he cast with concern. "Packy OK?"

"Can't you feel the difference between us?" I cast.

"Yes, Hap feel it, but was always that way," he cast back.

"It's a mystery, Hap, a real mystery."

"Maybe, but we need to move on. Did Packy hear the screaming last night?"

"Screaming?"

Once again a cold chill coursed through me.

"Tracker found us. The bull kept him away. Hap could see them from the ridge. Tracker stayed across the field, screaming, trying to scare everyone. I watched until dawn, when you woke, then I slept awhile. Hap didn't want to worry Packy, as I knew we were well guarded."

"Hap, it's virtually impossible for Tracker to catch up with us. Impossible."

"Tracker did, though."

I turned and got back into the van. Hap jumped in, and I turned the van around and headed back down the freeway. I was skeptical for the first time at something Hap had told me—the bull guarded us? It was preposterous.

And it was impossible for Tracker to find us. There was no way a creature on foot could catch up with someone in a vehicle.

Either Hap was lying or we were dealing with something that had to be supernatural, which would go against all I believed.

I drove on, deeply disturbed and more than a bit afraid, afraid of Tracker and also of what I had discovered about Hap—that he was so different from me, and that he had to be lying.

CHAPTER 19

We were soon near Butte, where we met up with I-90 and turned west towards Missoula, but only after getting more gas. I was now resorting to things like coasting down hills and trying to stay at about 55 m.p.h., trying to conserve fuel. But this big van was a real gas hog, no doubt about it.

It occurred to me that there was no way we were going to make it to the Canadian border unless I soon bought a gas can and siphon hose. This was a sobering thought, primarily because I hated stealing things, in spite of my track record so far on this trip. It felt like I was getting into this thing deeper and deeper.

We came to a freeway exit called Jens, and I pulled off and drove down a gravel road until we came to a bridge over the Clark Fork River. I needed a break, and I suspected Hap could use one, too, even though he was sleeping.

I didn't want to have him tell me he needed to stop when we got to Missoula. I'd been through there several times, and for some reason that town always seemed hectic.

I pulled down by the river a bit, into the willows where we wouldn't be as likely to be seen, then got out and stretched my legs.

The Clark Fork was a pretty river, not really all that big, lined with willows and huge old cottonwoods. It made me think of Colorado, and I was suddenly homesick.

I sat down on a log and watched the water ripple across the rocks, shining in the afternoon sun. Suddenly, I just wanted to forget everything and stay right there, live there on the banks of that river, it seemed so peaceful and carefree.

How did I ever get involved in this escapade, and why? How many times was I going to ask myself that question until I figured a way out? What was holding me to it?

There was no real reason I had to continue. I could just ditch the van and walk back up to the freeway and hitch a ride, go back east to Butte and have breakfast in one of the casinos there, then use what was left of my money to hop a bus back to Colorado or even on down to New Mexico or wherever I wanted to go, start a new life.

I can't tell you how badly I wanted to drop all this, and I also can't tell you why I continued on. I really don't know. Maybe I felt some sense of loyalty to Hap, or maybe it was just curiosity—I wanted to see how this all played out.

But maybe it went deeper, back to the reason I went back to that damn cave in the first place. I needed answers, even though I really didn't know what the questions were.

I finally woke Hap up, and he got out and walked around a bit, then squatted down and drank from the river. He then sat next to me and started eating willow leaves. He stripped off a bit of bark and started chewing on it, then spit it out and chewed on a new piece.

"What's up with the bark thing, Hap?"

"Hap have a headache, Packy, and the bark helps. Hap not sleep so good in the moving box."

I later found out that willow bark contains salicylic acid, the origin of aspirin. This wouldn't be the last time Hap would reveal an extensive knowledge of medicinal and edible plants, making me realize that though we humans may have technology, Bigfoot has a deeper knowledge of nature and our planet.

I cast, "Seems to me you sleep OK in the car, you seem pretty conked out."

"Maybe, but Bigfoot move around in their sleep, and Hap can't move in the moving box. Hap miss nest."

"You sleep in a nest?"

"Yes. Out in the forests, Hap make nest. Bigfoot like nest. Sometimes Bigfoot will even nest in a tree, when things are dangerous."

"When things are dangerous? What would be dangerous to a Bigfoot, other than humans, Hap?"

"Mostly humans. But sometimes other Bigfoot."

"Like Tracker?"

"Yes. Tracker and those who are becoming more like humans."

We sat for awhile, watching the water flow by, then I cast, "Hap, I'm lost."

"No, we're on track, we're OK, Packy."

"No, Hap, that's not what I mean. I'm lost, I feel lost."

"Hap don't know lost, then."

"Don't you ever feel like you're all alone on the edge of something really immense, like looking up at the stars, and you feel lost?"

"No," Hap replied.

"Never?"

"No. Why feel lost when you're always home?"

I cast, "You're a ranger. Your people are rangers. We humans, well, we used to be like that more, but now we've become domesticated, just like a dog. I know your kind ranges maybe too much, but there's something to be said for seeing at least a bit of the country."

"Hap don't know domesticated."

"Consider yourself lucky. See, Hap, I want to be away from my own kind. They disappoint me, embarrass me, fail me, all of that, and I just want to be far away from them all. But then when I am, I feel lost and lonely. But when I go back, I feel claustrophobic, closed in. I hate being indoors, I want to go outside and feel the wind in my face, see the night sky hanging there in its splendor. But then when I'm outside, far away from towns or other people, I feel lost."

"Hap don't know how to help Packy."

"I don't think there's a cure, Hap. It's like I have some long ago gene that humans once had and discarded, except for me, that is. I still have it. I don't fit in. I'm lost. I want a home, but I can't have one."

"Hap no understand, Packy, we cast about this before. Bigfoot who are lost, they sometimes end up like Tracker. Lose their roots. Tracker's seen too much. It made Tracker crazy. Bigfoot need home, but the Book of Runes says we must range."

We both sat there for a bit, enjoying the sound of the water and the cool shade. But suddenly, Hap stood and started for the van while casting to me.

"Packy, Tracker's nearby. He's casting to me. He wants me to answer so he can find us. Let's go."

I was skeptical. My doubts were growing that Hap was being honest.

"How could Tracker have possibly caught up to us again?"

"Hap don't know, Packy. We go."

I wanted nothing more than to stay right where we were, but the urgency in his thoughts gave me pause, so I got back into the van.

As we drove back onto the freeway, I finally let my doubts get the better of me.

"Hap," I cast, "Your story about the bull last night seems ludicrous."

"Hap don't know ludicrous."

"A lie."

"Hap don't know lie."

"You know, when you change what's real into a story that's not the same."

Hap was silent for a long time, then finally cast, "Hap very sorry Packy feels that way. Why would Hap lie?"

"I dunno, Hap. Maybe to keep me in the game."

"Hap don't understand."

"I know, I know, You never understand squat. But the thought of a bull out there in that field protecting us from Tracker is ludicrous. It doesn't seem possible. In fact, beyond possible—totally impossible."

I was now tooling along pretty good on the freeway, not really paying much attention to my speed. I was beginning to feel duped, which made me mad.

"I may be a stupid human and you an intelligent Bigfoot, but you guys can only fool me for so long into being the toadie that carries your so-called sacred book. I mean, nobody even knows where it's supposed to be taken or what it says. This whole thing is ludicrous, a bunch of bull, just like that bull. How could you possibly communicate with a bull?"

At that moment, I noticed someone was coming up behind me, right on my bumper. At first, I thought it was another state trooper and I felt a moment of panic, but that moment was nothing like the one I felt when the vehicle came up alongside us.

There, looking out the back window of a small RV was a very large Bigfoot, a really mean-looking Bigfoot. And now, the driver, a heavyset man, was trying to run me off the road.

"Tracker," Hap cast.

"You were right all along, Hap. My apologies. It's definitely Tracker. He appears to have got himself a chauffeur."

Now the RV swerved in front of us, running us into the grassy borrow ditch alongside the freeway. I slammed on the brakes, and we came to a crunching stop.

I grabbed the pack from under the seat in one hand and my Glock in the other, not sure whether to run or stay and fight as the RV swerved and came to a stop about fifty feet down the road from us, still half in the freeway lane.

CHAPTER 20

I had my hand on the door handle and was ready to bail out and start running when a big dually pickup truck came out of nowhere, its tires screaming and leaving rubber on the asphalt as it tried to stop.

As I watched in horror, it caught the side of the RV's bumper, making the RV skid along a bit from the impact.

I didn't even think about it, but just drove out of the ditch and took off as fast as I could.

Once back on the freeway, I looked in my rear-view mirror just in time to see Tracker running up into the trees alongside the road. He was dragging one leg, and it looked like he might be injured.

I was having a hard time feeling sorry for him, and I wondered if the driver had made it through all that unscathed.

Now I could hear Hap, and he was making some kind of strange huffing noise.

"Are you OK?" I cast.

"Hap OK. Tracker be slower from now on."

"I hope so," I answered. "I wonder who in the world he got to give him a ride."

"Hap don't know, but rumor says Tracker make friends with humans. I think the rumor correct."

I drove on, but I soon began shaking. Seeing Tracker had upset me, and my PTSD was now acting up, and I worried about having a panic attack. I had to stop soon and do something to mellow myself back out. All this stress was getting to me.

I decided I would try to stay calm until we could get to Missoula, then I would find a place that had comfort food. I'd get a chicken-fried steak and some mashed potatoes and go sit somewhere quiet and eat, try to relax.

I couldn't afford to lose it right then, it was a bad place and time, not that any place or time are good. I started taking deep breaths, then exhaling slowly.

I managed to hold it together, and after we'd been on the road for awhile, Hap had eventually gone back to sleep, obviously unaware of my turbulent mental state.

There wasn't much he could've done about it anyway, except worry. And after awhile, the monotony of the road settled me down some, and I tried not to think about Tracker and what was going on.

How in the world could I ever see this through? I was a nutcase, and why I was now in a position of such importance to Hap and his people was beyond me.

I knew for a fact that I would eventually let them down, and yet I had to continue on, I couldn't stop. I knew deep inside that this thing wasn't about them at all, it was about me. I was doing this for myself, though I had no idea why.

We soon dropped down the big hill into Missoula, and I really hated the thought of stopping, but I wanted to get something hearty to eat. I was sick of junk food, I was tired, and I was feeling a strange sort of malaise. It was a combination of mental and physical fatigue.

I took the first exit and soon found myself right smack in the center of town, right in heavy stop and go traffic, exactly what I had feared. All I wanted was some food, but instead, all I could find were espresso shops and book-stores and specialty shops.

Before I knew it, I was losing it, shaking my fist at people who cut me off, honking my horn and cussing out pedestrians, and generally making an ass of myself.

"Packy OK?" Hap cast.

"Stay down, Hap. we're in a city, too many people. I'm about to lose it. And yeah, I know you don't know lose it, but it ain't pretty. Just stay down, dammit."

I didn't hear a peep from Hap after that. I soon found my way out of the downtown core and to a shopping mall. There were people and cars everywhere.

I saw a Kentucky Fried Chicken and went through the drive through, then pulled behind a Home Depot to eat. After that, I went into the store and bought a gas can and a hose to siphon gas.

I was feeling a bit better by the time we headed over the small pass that took us north from Missoula. I knew we would soon be at Flathead Lake. I had always liked it there and had spent many great days camping on its shores.

It was now getting late in the day, and I began to worry about a place to camp for the night. The lake had several state campgrounds, but there was no way I could camp there and risk Hap being seen.

We arrived in Polson, which sets on the south end of Flathead Lake. I could go either left or right, as either direc-tion would eventually take me around the lake and on to Kalispell.

I decided to go left—I now had a plan. We would go to the little town of Lakeside and then on up above it to Blacktail Mountain, where a small ski area sat.

There was plenty of thick timber up there we could camp in, and there wouldn't be anyone around this time of year. I'd camped up there once not real long ago and really liked it, until I'd been run off by a grizzly, that was.

It was almost dark by the time we got to Lakeside, and I turned there to head on up Blacktail Road. It was a ways up to the top, maybe fifteen miles or so, and a pretty good climb. I knew it would be wise to gas up again before starting.

I pulled out my wallet (actually, Terry Murphy's wallet) and counted the bills. I was down to less than two-hundred dollars, and it would take a decent chunk of change to fill the tank. And I needed to keep money for food, as I couldn't just go graze like Hap did.

We had hit the proverbial end of the road, Hap and I, and it looked like we would either have to abandon the van here or get to work employing other resources, that is, our siphon hose and gas tank.

I didn't like the idea of stealing gas, but I knew the exact place to start—the cop car sitting along the highway just across from us, where the cop sat waiting to ticket unwary tourists.

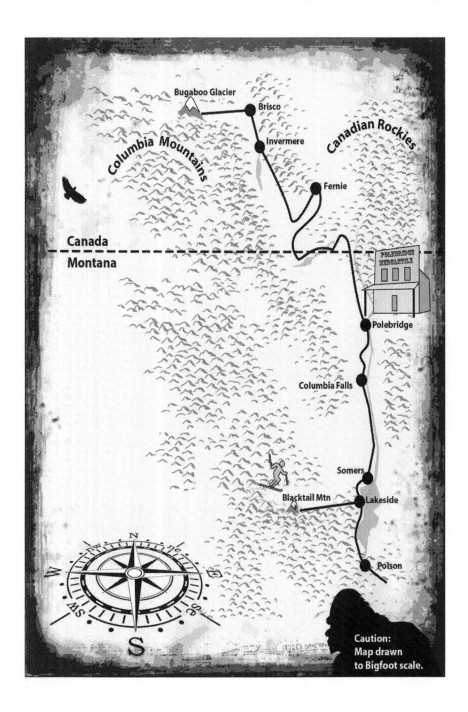

CHAPTER 21

As I mentioned, I had been in Lakeside before, just the previous year, to be exact. I remembered coming down the hill into town a bit too fast and at the last minute seeing that same cop sitting there on the side of the road.

It had really irritated me, but at least he hadn't given me a ticket. Now would be my chance to get revenge on behalf of all the tourists he'd scared the pants off in his speed trap.

I grabbed the hose and gas can from the back of the van, casting Hap to continue to stay down. It was almost dark, but we didn't need any Bigfoot sightings in the little town of Lakeside.

I snuck over to the edge of the highway, first hiding behind a little espresso shack, then trying to stay behind the few bushes that lined the road.

The cop was driving a black Ford Crown Victoria, and unfortunately, the car's gas tank was on the driver's side. I would have to be very careful that passing cars didn't see me.

I was soon crouched behind the car, watching the cop inside. He just sat there, making no movement, wearing a big cowboy hat and cop uniform, his face pale and drawn.

I smiled—there was no way he could catch me, but I knew his reinforcements would soon arrive and I would have to be quick.

I very quietly unscrewed the gas tank lid and slipped the siphon hose in. Even though I got a mouthful of gas, I soon had the gas can full and was on my way back to Hap and the van, half-running and ducking down, hiding behind things.

I quickly put the gas in the van's tank. I had managed to get a full five gallons, and I knew it wouldn't get us very far, but at least we'd make it up Blacktail and back down and maybe even on into Kalispell. This gas thievery would have to become a regular thing, as the van wouldn't go far on five gallons.

As I sat there in the parking lot, a pickup pulled up behind the cop car and a man got out of the truck's passenger side. He opened the driver's door of the Crown Vic and pushed the cop over into the passenger seat and then drove off, the pickup following. But they hadn't got more than a half-block when the cop car died—it sounded like it was out of gas.

I smiled, then turned onto Blacktail Road.

"Packy get food for the moving box?" Hap cast.

"Yup, but not very much."

"And the police, the one with the death flinger, he let you take it?"

"Yes, he made no move to stop me."

"Why not?" Hap cast.

"He's a dummy," I smiled. "The people of Lakeside don't have much money, so they bought an old cop car and a dummy and they set him by the road to make people slow down. Then at night, they take turns taking the car home for the night so it won't get vandalized. Then the next day, they take it back out. His name is Lucky, and he's a dummy."

"Lucky like Hap lucky? Packy says Hap lucky."

I laughed. "I dunno if having to sit by the road all day being a dummy is lucky or not, Hap. I found all this out when I was here last. The gal in the espresso shack told me all about him. Everyone thinks it's funny. There's an old saying that it's better to be born lucky than to be born rich, but in this case, I don't know."

I knew Hap didn't understand what I was talking about, but he let it go and didn't ask.

"Where now?" He cast.

I pointed up the hill we were now climbing, the thick trees along the road now just black shadows.

"We'll go up on top and you can find food while I sleep. Lots of thick forest and no people, but watch out for bears. Maybe you can round some up to guard us for the night."

I was kind of joking, but I couldn't help but still feel skeptical of Hap's bull story.

"Need pancakes," Hap moaned, ignoring me. He was apparently feeling sorry for himself.

"Hap, sweets are actually not good for you. Remember how you threw up?"

"Was from being in the moving box. Made Hap sick. Hap never throws up. Turn around. Hap knows stores have pancakes. Hap get us both some."

"You've been in stores?"

"No, but Hap's mother was in a store once."

"Where was that?"

"Somewhere by that big city we passed, the really big one before Hap got sick."

"Salt Lake City. What happened?"

"Hap's mother found a pan of stew on the window of a people box. She ate it. She thought it was for her, from nice humans. She stayed in the town for a week, thinking she was welcome, and even went into a store. But then humans started chasing her with death flingers. She hid so humans couldn't find her, then went back to the mountains."

I couldn't help but laugh. "Is this a Bigfoot legend or something?"

"Yes, she's famous, all Bigfoot know her story, and she's not afraid of humans. She has many stories."

"Hap, that's funny. I bet she was in South Weber. It's not far from Salt Lake City, up in the mountains. That story is now part of the South Weber urban legends. It's even on the internet."

"Hap don't know internet."

"Never mind. Look, we're home."

We had reached the top of the mountain, and I stopped by the locked gate to the Blacktail Mountain Ski Resort, the van lights shining on it through the darkness.

"Hap open gate," he offered, jumping out. Hap easily lifted the large metal gate off its hinges, allowing the van to drive through, then reset it. It looked like nothing had touched it.

I hadn't planned this, but I decided it was a great idea. What better place to be than inside of a locked gate? Nobody would bother us.

I was soon to find out otherwise.

97

CHAPTER 22

We drove on up the road, and I stopped in front of what looked to be a big building, and we both got out. The structure was three stories and painted yellow with rock facing along the bottom floor. I could make out the words, "Black-tail Mountain Ski Area" on the side. We had to be in front of the ski lodge.

Being from Colorado, I was used to ski areas that were at the bottom of the mountain, not on the top, but Blacktail Ski Area sat on the very top of Blacktail Mountain. I couldn't really see enough to know how it was all laid out, but I could see the far away lights of some city, probably Kalispell, and I could tell we were high above the valley.

It was a beautiful evening, and the stars hung low enough to reach out and touch, or so it seemed. It was weird, being in a ski area with nobody there and everything locked up.

I noticed a couple of lights on in the lodge, but I knew there was nobody there, they were just for security. Hap, who had apparently learned how to open doors from his legendary mom, went straight to the door.

"Hap, probably not a good idea for us to go in there. It would be trespassing." I knew what he was going to say, and sure enough, he said it.

"Hap don't know trespassing."

"It's when you go someplace that's not yours without permission."

"What is someplace that's not yours?"

"Well, you know, it doesn't belong to you."

"Hap don't know belong to you."

"Surely you have things that are yours, that belong to you, that nobody else can have or use without your permission?" I was getting exasperated again.

"No. Everything belongs to itself."

"OK, let's take this lodge. You go buy everything to build it, the lumber, the windows, the doors, all that kind of thing, then you pay someone to do the work."

"Hap don't know pay."

"It's when you do something for somebody and they give you something for doing it."

"You do it because you want to help. No need to pay."

"Oh man, Hap, how can I ever explain all this stuff? It's too complicated."

"Yes, humans are too complicated. Why build a lodge to start with?"

"So you can make money so you can pay for building more lodges."

I was feeling defeated. How could I ever make a simple creature who lived off the land understand the ways of humans who took things from the land and then charged each other to use them?

I cast, "Look, let's just forget it. I'm going to have a snack and then go to bed. You shouldn't have any trouble finding something to eat out here in all this wild forest."

"Pancakes." Hap looked longingly at the lodge.

"Hap, it's closed for the season. They wouldn't have anything to eat in there. Don't even try it. If you break in, they may have alarms and then someone with a death flinger will show up, and we'll have to hide. We don't need any more trouble. Stay out of there."

Hap looked disappointed, but soon disappeared into the thick timber nearby. I hoped to get a good night's sleep for once, as I suspected tomorrow would be a long day.

I wanted to reach the border, and I knew I would have to steal gas to do so, which would be very stressful, much more so than taking it from Lucky had been.

I actually had no idea how I was going to do all this and get us there, and once we got to the border, how could we possibly get across? These days, even the off-road areas were heavily watched by satellites and cameras and motion sensors.

I lay out my sleeping bag and pad on a grassy spot near the lodge and soon drifted off, only to be awakened by someone standing over me—someone very tall, very large, and with two ominous green eyes that shone like beacons through the black night.

As I held my breath and tried not to move, I saw two more sets of eyeshine, and three great beasts stood over me, all with green glowing eyes, and all very intimidating.

CHAPTER 23

"That's Packy, my friend. You won't want to harm or frighten him."

I could understand what Hap was casting, though it wasn't directed at me.

"You can't be friends with a human. It's forbidden in the Book of Runes," came a reply, once again not directed to me, though I clearly understood.

"Bigfoot is no longer bound to the book," Hap answered.

The three beasts didn't move and still stood above me, a feeling of menace emanating from them. I lay as still as I could, terrified.

The beast cast to Hap, "You cast sacrilege. You'll be killed if you continue."

The beast that was thoughtcasting was looking at Hap, who was standing in the shadows by the lodge. Now Hap stepped out, and I could see his eyes glowing red.

"Like I cast, you won't want to harm or frighten my friend. He has an important part in the future of the Bigfoot Nation. My name is Takoda, Friend to Everyone. You know me. Who are you?"

Now the trio stepped back. They seemed surprised and even intimidated.

"We are your friends, Takoda. We mean the human no harm, but how can you be friends when it is forbidden?"

The three Bigfoot stood back until Hap held out his arm, then one by one, they came up to him and performed what looked like a kind of handshake, except each would grab the elbow of the other in a firm hold, moving their long arms back and forth in unison, kind of swinging them.

The first came, grabbed Hap's arm, and cast, "My name is Akecheta, Warrior. I hold your arm with good feelings in my heart."

Then the second came. "My name is Chaska, Eldest Son. I hold your arm with good feelings in my heart."

Then the third. "My name is Tahatan, Hawk. I hold your arm with good feelings in my heart."

"Good. We now know one another and are in unity," Hap replied. "Come, and I'll introduce you to my friend."

By now, I was sitting up in my sleeping bag. Maybe I was having a strange dream, I thought. Hap and the trio came over next to me, and I stood, very aware of how small and puny I was next to these huge guys.

Hap cast, "This is my friend, Packy, Bearer of the Book of Runes."

The trio backed away from me and seemed shocked. Then Hap added, "He also bears a death flinger."

I knew Hap told them this to ensure my safety, knowing they wouldn't want to mess with someone with a gun, but I was perplexed at how he knew this. I hadn't mentioned the gun or shown it to him.

"How can our enemy be bearing our sacred book?" cast Akecheta. He seemed to be thinking about taking it from me—at least that's how I interpreted the look he gave me.

"The book's not sacred, Akecheta," answered Hap. "It was never sacred. It was a lie told by Erik the Red. The Greats have decided it's to be taken back to its origins and destroyed. It's caused the Bigfoot Nation much harm in its teachings, teachings like Bigfoot can't be friends with humans."

"And so, if the book is a lie made by humans, why would they not want us to be their friends?" asked Chaska.

"Erik the Red wanted to protect the Bigfoot. He knew humans are very destructive. But it would've been better if we had all been friends from the start. Now humans fear us and hunt us," Hap answered. "Those who believe in us, anyway."

"And carry death flingers," Chaska added, looking directly at me.

"Otaktay, Kills Many, is looking for us," Hap cast. "He wants the book, but I don't know why. Do you?"

I knew Hap was referring to Tracker.

"Rumor has it that he's befriended humans," Akecheta cast. "Just like you, Takoda." He sounded accusatory.

Hap answered, "My friend here, Packy, was chosen by the Elders to carry the book. Who are you to question the Elders?"

It was the first time I'd ever sensed Hap's anger, and it was thick in his casting. I worried that a fight might be brewing, but Akecheta quickly backed off.

"I'm a Bigfoot, Takoda, just like you and everyone else here, except him." He nodded towards me with what felt like disdain. "We answer to no one but ourselves, you know that."

I interrupted. "Then what good is the Book of Runes? Why do you follow it?"

The three Bigfoot looked shocked. Finally, Tahatan, who had been quiet until then, asked, "He can thoughtcast?"

Hap replied, "Yes." He then added, "Packy, we've been taught the book since we were babies. We may think we're independent and do things however we want, but deep inside the book guides us. It will be hard to unlearn it all, and it may not even be possible. And our children may still feel its influence, but once the book is destroyed and the Bigfoot Nation comes to understand how bad it's been for us, it will gradually lose its hold on us."

"What's in it that's so bad?" I asked.

"What you just heard about humans being our enemy, for example. Many of us fear humans because of that, and yes, it's true, some humans have flung death at us and tried to destroy us. Those Bigfoot who have been the object of such violence don't like humans and have sometimes been violent in return. But peace is the best way."

Now Tahatan spoke. "Kill me if you like, but I've never liked the book, but I was always afraid to say anything. The book taught us how to make fire. Fire has been very bad for us. Bigfoot gets soft sitting by a fire when it's cold, our coats don't thicken out like they should in winter. And we've burned down many forests with fire, killing many of our kind. Thankfully, the humans have put out most of the fires, or who knows how far they would have spread? And why must we range? It never made sense to me."

I cast, "It sounds like something a Viking would make up. They were explorers and loved to range."

Now everyone was quiet. Finally, Akecheta asked, "Takoda, your family brought us the book. If it's so bad, you are to blame."

Hap stood in silence for a moment, then cast, "Yes, Akecheta, that's true about my family, but I'm not responsible for what my family did, only for what I do. They meant no harm and were lied to, told it would be good for Bigfoot to follow the book. They didn't ask to be made heroes. I don't think Erik the Red meant harm either—he truly believed it would help. But Bigfoot are not humans, our ways are different, and the Red thought we would do better being like his people, which shows his lack of understanding."

Hap paused, then continued. "My legacy will be to destroy, with Packy's help, what my family brought." He nodded at me. "What future generations think about it all will be for them to decide—they can see me as a hero or as a villain, but the truth will be somewhere in the middle. In the meantime, I will do what I deem best and continue."

"Can we see the book?" asked Chaska.

I instinctively cringed. What if they decided to take it? Could my little Glock and Hap keep three huge giants away? I doubted it.

But then I thought about it—who cared, anyway? They would be doing us a favor, unless it got in the wrong hands, like Tracker's, though I had no idea what he would do with it.

"Packy, please get the book," Hap said.

I got my pack from beneath the van's seat and took out the Book of Runes. The trio were now standing back a bit, as if they believed all they'd heard about dying if you looked at it. This irritated me—I'd seen this same behavior all too often among my own superstitious species.

I opened the book, holding it out to them, but they seemed afraid of it.

"If it were truly sacred, wouldn't I be dead by now?" I asked.

Finally Chaska bravely came forward and took the book. He sat on his big haunches and slowly started thumbing through it, fascinated, and soon Akecheta and Tahatan were there, looking at it and gingerly touching the pages.

Hap even sat down by them, doing the same, and I realized he had only touched it that one time we looked at the maps. I knew he was fighting his own deeply held beliefs.

"While you're all checking it out, why don't you figure out the maps," I cast. "Hap, show them the maps. I want to see if I can get into the lodge."

Hap carefully took the book, opening it to the maps, oblivious to what I had just said about entering the lodge. Even though I had admonished him for wanting to break into the building, I now felt I had no choice but to do the same.

But I wasn't interested in finding food, I had a more urgent task in mind. I needed to destroy something—something that would incriminate me and my giant hairy friends and perhaps change the course of history for the Bigfoot by providing proof of their existence.

I had just noticed a small red light glowing above the side door of the lodge. Closer inspection revealed a security camera pointed directly at where the four of us had been talking, where the four Bigfoot sat this very moment, looking through the Book of Runes.

CHAPTER 24

I didn't know much about security systems—well, actually I knew basically nothing about them—but I did know that they had to record what they saw to some kind of media, whether it be an internal storage chip of some kind or via a signal sent to a phone or computer.

I watched the camera above the door and soon discovered that it seemed to have a motion sensor, for when I moved, the little red light would come on, and when I stopped it would go off after a few seconds. It was high above the door, completely out of my reach, and I knew it had to be sending a signal somewhere.

I had to get inside the building to figure out where that somewhere was, unless it was someone's phone, but I doubted very much if there were a good cell signal here.

I needed to get inside, yet I didn't want to trigger any possible alarms. Man, at this point I had not only stolen someone's money and ID, but also a vehicle and gas, was trespassing on the ski area's property, and was about to break-in and enter. If I ever got caught and charged with all this, I was looking at some serious prison time.

I was stymied. There was no way I could get inside without breaking something. I walked around the building a bit, but saw no way in. I needed help.

"Hap," I cast. He was still sitting with the trio, where they appeared to be engrossed in the book. He looked up, then came over.

"I need to get inside, Hap."

"Why?"

"See that little camera up there? That's been record-ing everything we've done. I know you don't understand camera or record, but it will show everyone Bigfoot exists. I have to get inside so I can deal with it."

Hap looked up at the smooth walls of the lodge. On the second story above, I could see a window was open a crack, but there was no way I could reach it—but maybe Hap could.

He cast to the trio that we needed help, and soon Chaska had climbed up the smooth wall and had the win-dow open. They were like a bunch of monkeys, the way they could climb, especially for how large they were. It was amazing. They couldn't possibly weigh as much as they looked.

Hap now leaned forward and cast for me to get on his shoulders, which I did. I still wasn't high enough, but he then got on the shoulders of Chaska and I was right there at the window and crawled in. It was kind of like being in a circus—a wild and crazy circus.

Breaking and entering with the help of a bunch of mythical nonexistent beasts would sure be hard to explain to a judge.

It was dark inside, but I soon found a light switch. I wanted to be quick, for if the camera was broadcasting a signal to someone down in town, my time was limited.

I wandered around a bit, finding nothing, then headed for the third floor. That was the most likely place for an office, I hoped, and sure enough, I was right.

Inside a small room were two desks, both with computers. One was turned on, as I could see a green light on the CPU. I touched the keyboard and sure enough, the monitor lit up.

On the screen was a folder with the flashing words, "Logitech Alert." Bingo, this had been too easy, and I knew the folder would contain the latest recording. I clicked on it and opened it, and sure enough there was a little icon with today's date and time on it.

But before I watched the video it contained, I needed to make sure there wasn't more being recorded. I cast Hap, hoping he would hear me.

"Hap, take down the camera. Rip it off. Can you hear me?"

"Yes, Packy. OK, it's down. I just tore it off. What should I do with it?"

"Just hang onto it for now. Actually, throw it into the van."

I now knew the camera could no longer record anything, so I started watching the video. It took a moment, but it soon loaded, and I watched with great interest.

It showed the van driving up and parking, then me getting out and putting my sleeping bag and pad on the ground.

The camera seemed to have pretty good night vision, for everything was very clear, almost like in the daytime, and it also had a good range of coverage—it looked to be almost 180 degrees.

The video stopped, then started again. It had shut off when I went to sleep, then turned back on when the trio had arrived. But even though the camera was recording, there didn't seem to be anything going on. I still lay on the ground, sleeping, but something had triggered it.

Now it showed me on my elbows, looking up. This went on for awhile, then I suddenly stood and kicked the bag off from around me. The video continued, even though I stood there motionless, then it showed me going to the van and getting out the Book of Runes.

I was perplexed, as it seemed like the Bigfoot weren't showing up. Maybe it was because they were dark, but if it were a night-vision camera, it should at least show their body heat, making them look like ghosts—or show those glowing eyes.

I sat there a bit longer, then watched the most surreal thing I've ever seen. I reached out to hand the book to Hap, but he wasn't there, yet something took it. The book was now floating in thin air, and I could see the pages being slowly turned. It was creepy.

I sat there in front of that monitor for a moment in shock, then closed the video and dragged it into the computer's trash. I had the presence of mind to empty the trash and then check for more videos, but there was nothing with that day's date on it, so I knew I had deleted the only possible evidence of our visit.

Except it wasn't much evidence at all, unless one wanted evidence of strange books that float in thin air.

I stood and walked down the stairs to the bottom floor, leaving the lights on as I went, unlocking the front door.

I walked out, cast to Hap that we needed to go, bravely went and took the book from Chaska, got in the van, and started it up.

Hap didn't even have time to get in, but he managed to catch up at the closed gate, where he opened it and barely jumped in before I was headed back down Blacktail Road in a daze.

I had decided I had gone insane and needed help, even though I had no idea who to ask. Maybe the linguistics prof could help me—assuming I could somehow get ahold of him.

CHAPTER 25

"What's wrong, Packy?" Hap cast.

"Shut up, Hap. You're not real, so just shut up."

"Hap don't know real, Packy."

"I know you don't. Look, Hap, I'm having a meltdown, OK? I can't figure any of this. I'm probably sitting in some lunatic asylum right now, muttering to myself, and the nurse is on her way with the meds."

I was going dangerously fast down the windy gravel road, but I didn't care. Nothing seemed real any more, and I had totally lost my bearings.

"Hap still hungry, Packy. Didn't get to eat since the other Bigfoot there. Can we stop here in the trees for awhile?"

"So, what's with the weird names?"

"What?"

"You know, weird names. Chaska, Akecheta, Tahatan, and you're Takoda. I know these kinds of names. They're weird crap people make up when they're living in a fantasy world, like in some sci-fi novel. Nobody has names like that, not really. That's what tipped me off, the names. See, you can't fool me, I know I'm insane. You're not even real, you're a figment of my whacked-out imagination."

"I dunno, Packy. They're just our names. Our family called us that."

"They sound like something from a tribe up in Alaska or something, stuff where everyone sits around trying to make up crap that sounds real, like for a book or something. Problem is, it sounds phony as hell. It's not real."

"I'm sorry, Packy. Can we stop?"

My lights caught a small side road, and I came to a screeching halt, then turned down the little two-track into the thick trees.

After about a hundred feet or so, I stopped and killed the engine and got out. The road ended in a small clearing, a camp spot.

"OK, here's dinner, go for it. Don't be gone long if you want a ride with me, even though I know you're just a figment."

Hap jumped out and was instantly gone. Just then, I saw a vehicle going up the road we'd just come down, and I knew it was someone checking on the security camera. They couldn't see us in the trees. Luckily I'd pulled off when I did.

I leaned against the van, wondering what was going on. The video had showed nary a trace of Bigfoot, and I'd panicked, once again doubting my own senses and eyes.

This was typical for me, I had more self-doubts than not. I'd always been that way, unable to trust my own instincts when it came to anything but survival in the wilds. There, I was pretty competent—it was the only place I'd ever felt safe.

But I'd known that there were numerous cases of people with cameras who had seen Bigfoot but hadn't been able to get a photo—blobsquatches, is what people called the fuzzy and blurry images, if they got any image at all. So why be surprised that the camera on the lodge hadn't been any more successful, given the general track record?

Was it really me, was I going insane, or was it something to do with Bigfoot? Did it have to do with what I'd been thinking about earlier, their physical makeup? Was there something about them that the human eye could see but the camera couldn't?

It didn't make sense. Cameras capture light waves, as does the human eye. Why would the eye be able to capture something a camera couldn't? I knew from experience that the human eye saw things differently from the camera, something anyone who tries to capture a scene would attest to.

This is why photographers had to study f-stops and such, the amount of light a lens lets into the camera, so they could make their images look more like what the eye actually saw. It was a fine and difficult art, as the human eye could see much more than a camera in terms of contrast and shades.

But there were also cameras that captured light waves the human eye couldn't see, like infra-red. Was it possible that the human eye could see wavelengths nobody suspected, wavelengths that Bigfoot radiated or emanated or whatever it was and cameras couldn't?

"Hap," I cast. "Are you around?"

"Over here."

"Why do some Bigfoot have green eyes and some red?"

"Dunno, Packy. Why do some humans have green eyes and some blue or brown or red?"

"How do you know that?"

"I dunno. My mom told me."

"Everything but red. Are you finding anything to eat?"

"Lots of nice ferns here."

"Hap, can you guys project light from your eyes, like a flashlight?"

"I don't know flashlight, but yes, we can make light come from our eyes."

"How do you do it?"

"I dunno, Packy. You just make it go on when you want, like the bad smell."

"Some deep water fish can do that. So, you do have scent glands?"

"We can make bad smells, yes. It's a defense."

"Just like a skunk, except Bigfoot cologne."

"Don't know skunk or cologne."

"Sure you do, a little animal, black with white stripes on its back, stinks to high heaven."

"OK, Hap know skunk. Squirts."

I laughed. "Hap, I'm gonna sleep. Is it safe here? Are your weird buddies coming down here?"

"It's safe, Packy. Hap keep watch."

With that, I crawled into the back of the van. If I were indeed nuts, a little sleep would help clear my mind before the doctor came and got me for shock therapy.

I slept like a baby, not waking until dawn, nor do I remember having any dreams.

CHAPTER 26

When I woke, I was stiff and sore. I'd gone to sleep sitting in the driver's seat, though I would swear I'd been in the back.

But Hap was in the back, snoring, the sheets pulled over his head. He must've moved me somehow without waking me. I suspected he was afraid I would leave without him, so he'd crawled into the back. I must've been really tired to not wake up.

Or so I thought at the time. Later, after thinking about it some, I suspected that he'd been able to induce a deep sleep in me that wasn't entirely natural.

I'd read about this in Bigfoot encounters, people who had seen a Bigfoot and immediately became groggy and couldn't stay awake. I suspected the use of infrasound again, though I couldn't prove it.

"Hap, did you do something to make me sleep last night?"

There was no reply. I couldn't tell if he was avoiding me or actually sleeping.

I started up the van and headed back down the Black-tail Road to the little town of Lakeside, coasting most of the way to save gas.

It was about seven a.m. when I got to the parking lot of the Blacktail Market. I drove through the little espresso shack and got a latte with an extra shot.

The girl at the shack was amiable enough, and I asked her if she knew the directions to Bowman Lake, which was up in Glacier National Park.

She didn't, and I suspected she didn't, and that's why I asked. As I drove off, I told her I would ask the cop over by the road, not giving her time to tell me he was just a dummy.

It's funny how the mind works—now that I had planted the seed, I hoped she would see me over there and think I was talking to the cop, even though she knew he was a dummy. We all operate on auto-pilot sometimes, some of us more than others.

I pulled up next to the cop car, the van hiding me and my work on the gas tank from anyone on the highway. I quickly got out my thief kit—the siphon hose and gas can. I was getting better at this, or at least more brazen, but I would have to work fast.

I soon had the five-gallon tank full and poured it into the van. I was working on pure adrenaline, and I was beginning to understand why some people stole things they didn't need—it was the adrenaline rush. It made you feel alive—way more alive than I wanted to feel, actually.

The more gas I could get now, the better. I filled the can three more times before I hit bottom. I had stolen all of Lucky's gas, about 20 gallons—they'd obviously filled it last night after running out. Poor Lucky. He'd be walking again tonight—well, theoretically, anyway, since he was a dummy.

I jumped in the van and took off, slipping out of the little town before anyone noticed. We would work our way

around the north end of Flathead Lake and head towards
Canada, though I still had no idea how we would get across
the border.

We soon reached the little town of Somers, where I
pulled onto a back lane that led out into the countryside.
I got out, poured some water from a water jug onto the
ground, then took the mud I'd just made and smeared it
onto the van's license plates. I then tried to make it look
natural by smearing more mud onto the rear bumper and
wheelwells.

We were for sure on the stolen vehicle lists by now, and
I wanted to decrease our chances of getting stopped. The
mud would maybe prevent a cop from running our plates.

Now back on the highway, I cut across the top of Flathead Lake, which would let us avoid Kalispell and all the
people there. We were quickly going north again.

It was a beautiful area, with lots of big green fields and
open terrain marching up to thick forests of what looked
like old-growth spruce and fir. Hap seemed to be sleeping
soundly in the back, which was good.

Until he wasn't.

"Packy, Hap thirsty."

"Stay down, Hap. I'll find some water."

I hadn't been buying water anymore, as Hap went
through it too quickly. It was easier to find a pond or
stream. But we were now in a fairly populated area, so I'd
have to be careful.

I saw a sign that said Old Highway 35 and pulled onto
it. I then turned onto a road that appeared to climb into the
woods. I climbed and climbed into thick forest, until bingo,
there we were in a subdivision of empty lots right by a
small lake edged with timber.

"Here ya go, Buddy," I cast to Hap.

Before I could get out, he was down in the pond swimming and drinking. I kept an eye out for people, although we were pretty remote. The views of the Swan Mountains were stunning.

I watched Hap as he enjoyed the water, but then noticed he wasn't alone.

"Hap, there's an otter or something swimming in there, watch out."

"Not otter."

"What the heck is it?" I could see something paddling along behind Hap, something relatively small, though anything would look small beside him.

"Little Wagger."

"What the hell's a Little Wagger?" I had a sinking feeling I really didn't want to hear his answer.

"Has little tail that always wags."

"Where did it come from?"

"Lost at lodge."

"You found it up there?"

"Yes. Hungry."

"You're hungry and gonna eat it? Over my dead body, Hap. I don't know what it is, but you'd better not eat it."

"Hap not eat flesh." He sounded disgusted. "Little Wagger hungry. Packy need to feed it."

Hap was soon back at the shore, where a small dog followed him out of the water, dripping wet, bedraggled, and skinny. It was a yellow-brown color and looked to be a Terrier mix of some kind.

The little dog ran up to me, shaking and getting me all wet. But just then, something caught my eye up high over the trees.

"What is it?" Hap cast with fear.

"It's a hot-air balloon," I replied.

"Hap don't know hot-air balloon."

He slipped into the trees, but continued to watch and ask questions.

I cast, "You take fabric, put air in it so it floats, then tie a basket to it and ride in it."

"What's fabric?"

I held up my jacket. "This is fabric."

"What's air?"

I was frustrated. How do you explain something like air? Finally, I blew on a leaf. "That's air, wind."

The balloon spotted me and the people waved, and I waved back. It had soon drifted on over, and Hap came back out of the trees.

"This hot-air ballon is a human thing then?"

"Yes. Another human thing, but this time pretty harmless."

"You ride in it?"

"Yes, you can see everything from it. Like being on a mountain."

"Packy ever ride in it?"

"No."

"Dangerous?"

"I dunno, maybe sometimes, but I don't think they crash very often."

"Why do this?" Hap seemed puzzled.

"To see everything, be adventurous, I guess."

"Why not just climb a mountain?"

"Because you can be like a bird. You can fly. Haven't you ever wanted to fly, Hap?"

"No," he replied.

Hap now took my jacket from the van and started blowing into the sleeve, trying to fill it with air. I couldn't help but laugh at his childlike innocence. He had no idea what air was. But then I stopped and realized his innocence was maybe a blessing.

I was suddenly envious. I no longer wanted to know all the things I knew, I no longer wanted to be human. It seemed like a dreadful burden. I couldn't recall ever being innocent, and I could only vaguely imagine how sweet it must be.

I watched Hap as he swung my jacket through the air, then tossed it high into a nearby tree with his massive arms, trying to get it to float.

He then easily scaled the tree, climbing like a monkey, throwing the jacket back to me. It floated for a mere second, and as he watched, he started making a chattering noise, and I knew he was having fun like a little kid.

No wonder he was happy being Hap, I thought, wishing I could be more like him myself.

"Packy want to fly?" Hap asked.

"I don't give a flying rat's ass about flying. I did plenty of it in the war," I replied.

I couldn't help it, but I was suddenly angry—maybe a hint of my PTSD. I wasn't mad at Hap, but at my life, you name it, everything, mad that I couldn't get rid of all the bad memories and be happy, like Hap.

"Hap don't know war."

"You're lucky."

"Tell Hap."

"Well, it's like you have a bunch of Trackers on your side and I have a bunch on my side, and we all get together and fight and try to kill each other."

"Why?"

"I dunno, over say, huckleberries."

"Why?"

"There's not enough for everybody—or so they say—so we fight. But I think it has more to do with just not liking each other. We humans are just a bunch of monkeys, just like you guys."

I then remembered the little dog, who was now trying to climb my leg to get me to pick it up, which I did and was immediately all wet.

I groaned. This was all I needed, another mouth to look after and feed.

CHAPTER 27

"Look, Hap, we're gonna have to find an animal shelter for this little guy. He deserves a good home. We're going to reach the Canadian border today, and after that, we'll be on foot. We have no way to feed him."

"Hap feed Wagger."

"Hap, dogs don't eat weeds and ferns, like you do. They eat meat. Are you gonna kill animals so he can eat?"

"Packy feed Wagger."

"And who's gonna feed Packy?"

"Stores."

"There won't be any stores where we'll be going, Hap. We're gonna have to hide out, and we sure as hell won't be waltzing down any streets looking for grocery stores."

Wagger now came over to me, as if he sensed his future was in my hands. The poor thing looked totally starved, so I fed him some cheese I'd bought a couple of days ago. It was hard as a rock, but Wagger gulped it down.

"You poor little guy," I said while patting his head. "Where did you come from, way up on Blacktail—how'd you get up there?" I pulled some burrs from his coat.

Wagger sat quietly, as if he understood what I was doing, then held up his paw for a shake.

"Shake, Wagger, shake."The little dog was now wagging his tail and dancing around.

Hap showed his teeth."Wagger like Packy."

"Nice try, Hap. We're taking him to a shelter. We're going right through the town of Columbia Falls, so we'll stop there. He deserves better than walking through Canada with a big hairy ape and a depressed war vet, starving to death."

I got in the van, and Wagger jumped up into the passenger seat. Hap was soon settled in the back, under his sheets, and we headed back down the hill.

It didn't take long to get to Columbia Falls, our last real outpost before hitting the wilds. I'd studied the map and decided we should continue to follow the North Fork of the Flathead River on up into Canada. It seemed like the least travelled route.

The road became gravel after Columbia Falls, going through the tiny settlement of Polebridge, then on to a closed border crossing. We'd have to ditch the van before that point and cross on foot, and that would put us in the wilds of the Canadian Rockies.

That would also mean the last of any food sources for me. I'd have to learn to eat the same plants Hap subsisted on, if I could. I sure as hell wasn't looking forward to it.

Once in Columbia Falls, I stopped at a gas station and asked where the animal shelter was, but no one knew. After checking their phone book, I found that the nearest one was in Kalispell.

I really didn't want to drive all the way over there, but it looked like the thing to do, if I were going to find Wagger a good home. I headed west.

Suddenly, I pulled over. There was an A&W drive-in, and I couldn't think of anything that sounded better than a hamburger and fries. It was the old-fashioned kind of drive-in where you parked and ordered through a speaker and they brought your order to you.

"Hap, stay down," I cast, then placed my order over the little speaker—four hamburgers, two orders of fries, and a root-beer frosty. I hadn't had anything like this for so long, and it sounded really good. It didn't take long to get my order, and me and Wagger sat there together, happily munching away.

Just then, an old beat-up station wagon pulled in next to us. It was filled to the brim with kids all talking at the same time, while the dad was trying to get them to tell him what they wanted to eat. Maybe some kind of birthday party, I figured.

I was about ready to go when the kids started shrieking and screaming. I knew Hap had raised his head to see what was going on, in spite of being told not to.

"Dammit, Hap, stay down!" I cast, mad.

One of the kids yelled, "Hey, Mister, there's a gorilla in your backseat!"

Everyone started yelling and talking all at once.

One kid yelled, "Tell the gorilla to sit up so we can see him again."

Now the dad was trying to make them all calm down. He nodded at me in embarrassment. I smiled back as if to say it was OK, but I knew it was time to leave.

Now another kid yelled, "It ain't no gorilla, it's a man in a gorilla suit."

"Is not, it's a gorilla."

I put the van in reverse and started to leave, but a thought crossed my mind. These kids would make a perfect home for Wagger. I stopped and got out, putting Wagger under my arm, then walked over to the station wagon.

"I found this little dog and can't keep him. Any chance you guys would like to take him home?"

"We want to see the gorilla again," the kids replied.

"Oh, that's just my friend Eddie," I said. "He's on his way to a birthday party, dressed up in that suit. Isn't this little dog cute?"

Wagger wasn't wagging his tail any more and instead seemed scared.

"I'll have to ask my wife first," the man replied. "Can you give me a number where I can reach you?"

Now one of the kids was half-hanging out of the back window of the car, reaching for Wagger, who let out a sharp yelp. This was all it took for Hap to again show his face, and of course everyone saw him.

"That's not a gorilla!" One of the kids screamed. "It's a gorilla in a Bigfoot suit!"

I decided it was time to go, so I thanked the man and got back in the van, setting Wagger on the passenger seat and quickly heading out.

I could hear pandemonium behind me as the kids yelled for me to come back, but I just floored it and headed for Polebridge.

I knew Hap had intentionally stymied my efforts to find Wagger a home, and it made me mad.

"Hap," I cast. "Why did you do that?"

There was no answer.

Wagger had now curled up and gone to sleep, his tummy full of hamburger.

I didn't want to admit it, but I was secretly glad the little guy was still there, though I had no idea what I was going to do with him. I figured I'd cross that bridge when I came to it.

CHAPTER 28

I headed onto the road from Columbia Falls to Polebridge, again wondering where in the hell I was going. Right now, my main goal was to ditch the van and get across the Canadian border.

I knew there was no way I could get the van across, and without a passport, there was no way I could get myself across, not legally. It looked like I was about to add an illegal border crossing to my list of infractions.

I started humming "Folsom Prison Blues" as we drove along the wide gravel washboarded road that led north, following the scenic Flathead River.

Hap and Wagger both slept while I struggled with many questions, not the least being what I was doing there. My brain just couldn't turn that one off.

After some time, we finally reached the small town of Polebridge, which featured the Polebridge Mercantile as about its only business, though I think one could also rent cabins there.

I guessed that the mercantile's main business came from tourists to the far western edge of Glacier National Park and the campgrounds at Bowman and Kitla lakes. The whole town was run on generators, as they didn't have electricity.

I pulled over across the road from the store, as I didn't want any more shenanigans from Hap, people seeing him and all that. I told him to stay down or he'd get shot, and I was about ready to do the deed myself. I went into the old-fashioned general store to get supplies for the journey across the border.

I was kind of kicking myself for not doing this in Columbia Falls where things would be cheaper, but after the incident with the kids seeing Hap, I had just wanted to get out of town.

The minute I opened the door, I knew I was a goner from the smell. Every square inch of the store was lined with tourist stuff, things like postcards, but what really made the place so popular was their bakery and deli.

And since huckleberries are plentiful in Montana, the store capitalized on that fact and sold tons of huckleberry stuff— huckleberry bearclaws, sticky rolls, muffins, jams, pancake syrup—along with stuff like chili corn bread and cheese jalapeño bread.

I thought about buying Hap some of the pancake syrup, but knowing him, he would just drink the bottle all at once and get a sugar buzz. Speaking of Hap, I hoped he didn't smell the berries and decide to come check the place out. That would be a disaster.

I bought a turkey sandwich and a big bag of huckleberry baked goods, as well as bread and jerky and some canned stuff, like spam.

The place was crammed with tourists, and I had to wait in line. Oddly enough, ahead of me in the line were two young guys who looked to be in their late teens and just happened to be talking about Bigfoot, of all things.

"Man, you'll never understand until you've seen one yourself. I just can't describe how scary they are."

"Where did you see one?"

"Out in Ohio at Salt Fork State Park. I was with my brother—it was huge, dude. Later, we heard that a guy was going around hoaxing people in a ghillie suit, but I doubted it."

"You mean a gorilla suit."

"No, a ghillie suit. It's different. It's military—what they wear to hide in the jungle."

"Oh. But why didn't you believe you'd been hoaxed? I mean, if the guy admitted to it..."

"Look, dude. Would you believe someone who had confessed to being a hoaxer? Someone like that can't be trusted at all, they're liars. So I know what we saw was the real deal."

I paid for my stuff, then went back out to the van, wondering what the pair would think if they knew there was a real live genuine Bigfoot in the parking lot, not far from their car.

"Hap smells berries," Hap cast.

"Stay down. I bought you some berry pancake stuff. We'll stop once we get away from people. Just stay down."

Wagger was sitting on the seat looking out the window, wagging his tail at everyone. I once again felt a pang of pain for the little dog. I had no right to make him trek across the Canadian Rockies with me—he deserved a good home, even though I was getting really attached to him.

I headed onto the dirt road going north, and I knew we would soon be at the border. I felt a combination of tension and fear and excitement of the unknown, and I knew we would soon have to figure out a way across, and it would have to be on foot.

Even though this area was pretty remote, I did see an occasional house in the woods, what I figured had to be summer homes. After driving a few miles, I pulled over on what appeared to be a long driveway up to someone's house, even though I couldn't see the house itself.

Hap was wanting pancakes, so this would be a good place to stop and take a break. I'd keep an eye out for anyone coming down the lane.

Hap got out of the van, and I handed him the sack of baked goods, after grabbing a sticky roll for myself.

"Don't eat them all at once, Hap. You've been down that road before and know exactly where it goes."

Hap showed his teeth and took the sack. I let Wagger out and fed him part of my turkey sandwich, then gave him some water in my coffee cup. He wolfed it all down, even though I knew he was still full of hamburger. He seemed grateful and wagged his tail.

Hap handed me back the empty sack, then cast, "Hap go for a snack."

He hadn't been gone for more than a few minutes when I saw a car coming up the road. I grabbed Wagger and waited, and soon an older gray-haired woman driving a blue Mercury Mystique stopped, with a person who looked like he could be her husband in the passenger seat.

"Hello. Are you looking for someone?" she asked.

I answered, "No, I just stopped here off the main road a bit to let my little dog out."

She smiled, then replied, "I thought I heard you say something, but didn't quite catch it."

It had been so long since I'd talked to someone that I realized I'd thoughtcast to her.

I now spoke the words, "I just stopped here to let my little dog out. My name's Sam. Hope I'm not disturbing anything."

"No, you're fine. We live on up the road and rarely see anyone out here, so we were just wondering if all was OK. That's sure a cute dog."

"Isn't he though? He's a stray. I found him up on Black-tail Mountain over by Lakeside. I can't keep him and am looking for a good home for him. Would you be interested?"

The woman held out her hand and Wagger started licking it. This was a good sign, I figured. I really didn't want to part with him, but I feared what lay ahead. A nice gentle couple like this would be the perfect home.

"Oh my, he's a little doll. Needs to be fattened up a little, though. What do you think, Harry?"

She turned to her husband. He was smiling and nodding his head submissively.

"Is it a boy?" she asked.

"I think so," I replied, kind of holding him up to look. "Yep, a boy, just as I thought. You guys would give him a good home? He's a real sweet dog, smart as a whip, and I want him to be happy."

"Oh certainly," the woman replied. "We have another dog, a little Shih Tzu, and they would be best friends. Let's take him, Harry. What did you say his name is?"

"Wagger, but you can call him anything you want."

I handed Wagger to her through the window. He struggled a bit, not sure about the state of things, but she handed him to her husband, who started petting him, and

Wagger seemed to settle down.

"You folks are sure good-hearted," I said. "I'll be on my way now. Say, though, have you ever been across the border on up this way?"

Harry answered, "No, we always go on over to the main highway at Roosville to cross. It's nothing but back roads here, and I think the crossing is closed now."

"Do they patrol it much? I mean, if one were to go hiking and accidentally cross over, would you get in trouble?"

Harry looked concerned.

"If you accidentally cross over, you're gonna be real sorry," he said. "They don't take too kindly to accidental border crossings."

"That's what I figured," I said. "I think I'll head south and hike down there. Maybe go to Kintla Lake."

"That sounds like the prudent thing to do," the woman replied. "This is our summer home, and we're leaving soon to go to Arizona. We'll take little Wagger here on up to the house and introduce him to Fanny May—after a bath and some perfume, of course. You don't mind if we change his name, do you? Little Prince would be cute."

She smiled and slowly started up the road.

I'll never forget the look of betrayal on Wagger's face as the couple took off, the little dog sitting on Harry's lap, his head turning to watch me until they were out of sight.

The look on Wagger's face was rivaled only by that same look of betrayal on Hap's face after he returned from his snack and I explained where Wagger was off to.

And if I'd had a mirror, I would have seen the look on my own face of someone who had made a big mistake, a mistake that couldn't be rectified, even though I had only been trying to do what was best for Wagger.

CHAPTER 29

I drove on a ways, feeling kind of sick. Every once in awhile I felt a tinge of anger from Hap, as if he were trying not to let on but couldn't help it anyway.

We rode in silence on up the windy dirt road that was beginning to feel more and more remote, as we'd left most of the tourists far behind at Polebridge.

I did some thinking in the silence, especially about my thoughtcasting to the woman and her almost getting it. I wondered if humans hadn't at one point been able to cast to each other, long before we'd developed speech.

It seemed like casting for me was getting easier, and if I concentrated more on images and pictures while doing it, Hap understood me more clearly.

It was the abstract concepts that would hang us up, things like love or lying—moral and emotional constructs. The other things that always threw us off were when I was trying to tell Hap about something cultural or technological—he usually didn't get it at first, if at all.

We finally came to a side road called Trail Creek Road, and I turned onto it. The sun was beginning to fade into the horizon, and I wanted to find a place to camp, get lots of rest for our border crossing the next day.

The Flathead River Valley has been called the Serengeti of the North because it has so much wildlife—bighorn sheep, moose, wolverines, elk, and the highest density of grizzly bears in the interior of North America.

But for all the time we spent there, I swear I saw fewer animals than I did on a good day back home in Colorado, and after awhile, I had to suspect that it had something to do with traveling with a Bigfoot. It seemed like the woods were quiet when Hap was around.

After a bit, I found a little two-track going back into the trees and pulled off. There was so little traffic here that I didn't worry much about anyone coming along. I turned the van around and parked under some tall Western red cedars.

I got out and walked around, noting a small fire ring. Someone had camped here before, and they'd even left a bit of wood split and ready for the fire.

I ate a can of spam, sat around for awhile, then finally made a fire. Hap was long gone, out foraging for the night, and the place seemed really remote. I felt lonely and wanted the fire for comfort.

I was now missing Wagger and wishing I hadn't been so stupid as to give him away, especially to someone who would treat him more like a kid or a toy than like a dog.

I knew Wagger would hate that, being a descendent of the Venerated Order of Wolves—or at least that's how I looked at dogs, members of a species that had been smart enough to acclimate themselves to humans for survival. And DNA showed that dogs descended directly from wolves.

After all, biologists believed that wolves domesticated themselves, not the other way around with humans domesticating the wolves, as we'd believed for years.

It seems that wolves began scrounging at human garbage dumps and gradually became tamer and tamer, the humans encouraging their company for protection.

Anyway, Wagger sure wasn't no wolf, but I did feel better having him around. It was another set of eyes and ears, both of which were much better than mine. And I enjoyed his company—he was a smart little beggar.

As I sat by the fire, I thought of many things, Tracker not being the least, as well as the trio up at Blacktail with the weird names. I guess I'd given up on figuring out if I were sane or not. I'd just have to be what I was and hope it all worked out.

I sat there for a long time, thinking of our journey so far and wondering what the future held. I was tempted to get the Book of Runes out to once again study the maps, but I knew they wouldn't show anything new.

That night would be my last night in the United States, my last chance at an easy escape from all this, this burden that had somehow become my lot in life against my wishes. I could leave the book under a tree, turn the van around, go back and get Wagger and head back to Kalispell, where I could hide the van in some trees and hitch a ride back to Colorado. There was nothing to connect me to that van in any way, as I'd used a fake ID to rent it. I could go back to my former life.

I can't tell you how tempted I was, but something held me there. Maybe it was a new loyalty I was beginning to feel to Hap, a feeling of not wanting to let him down.

Also, it was the first time since before the war that I'd had a purpose or any meaning, and maybe that was it, too. And I had no idea what my role in all this was, but according to Hap, it was critical to the fate of his kind. Maybe I was being conned, but if not, well, I just couldn't go there, couldn't let them down.

The fire was beginning to burn itself out, so I finally kicked dirt onto it and crawled into my sleeping bag in the van. I was tired and depressed, and I realized it was my own fault, as I was missing Wagger. I hoped the little dog was OK and enjoying his new life. It sure as hell would be a lot more stable and secure than with me.

I slept deep, then woke sometime in the night, dreaming that Wagger was down in my sleeping bag with me, smelling vaguely of a strange mix of perfume and Bigfoot musk. I smiled as I turned over and went back to sleep, dreaming the little dog was licking my arm.

I would wake in the morning, Wagger there by my side, Hap sleeping in a makeshift nest under the trees, and I would realize it hadn't been a dream after all. Hap had apparently taken it upon himself to rescue the little dog, and I couldn't have been more pleased.

It would be a turning point in the journey, a decisive fulcrum for what was to come, for it would somehow make me realize that what I did really mattered, really did make a difference in the lives of others.

This would give me a sense of empowerment, something I hadn't felt for years, though I hate that word, as it smacks of self-help crap. And it would also be the end of my PTSD and many of my self-doubts.

But it's true, it was the turning point for us all—me, Hap, and even Wagger. We were now a team, a true team with a common goal—though Wagger may not have realized we had a goal. But we were all part of something bigger than ourselves.

Little did I know what was in store for us, nor what an important part I would play in our adventure—nor did I realize that the real journey had just begun.

CHAPTER 30

The next day, after sharing another can of spam with Wagger for breakfast and longing uselessly for a huckleberry roll, I tried to clean up and bury anything in the van that might serve as evidence, such as food wrappers and things that might have my fingerprints on them.

I took the sheets Hap had been using and buried them a ways off, and when I found the security camera from the Blacktail Lodge, I threw it in a nearby pond.

I had the pack with the Book of Runes in it all ready to go, my sleeping bag and pad tied to it, and food crammed down around the book.

I sat down on a big log, already tired at the thought of what was to come. Hap was nowhere to be seen, and Wagger lay at my feet as if he knew something was about to change in a big way.

As I set there, I got more and more paranoid. I thought about the possibility of going to jail for car theft. I needed to get rid of the evidence better—I knew there were dozens of fingerprints all over that van.

I eyed the pond, wondering how deep it was, then decided to give it a try. I got in and drove the van to the edge of the pond, then jumped out at the last minute as it slowly continued on.

I watched with great satisfaction as it sank into the water, gone. It had been a nice vehicle but could've been my ticket to jail, but no more. It was totally submerged.

Now we really were on our own and there was no going back. I went and sat on the log again, waiting for Hap, wondering where we'd be by nightfall, and if we could successfully cross the Canadian border or not.

It wasn't long before Hap showed up, puzzled by the missing van. I tried to explain why fingerprints could be evidence against me, but I knew he didn't understand, so I let it go. I was too tired to try to explain it all—fingerprinting, locking people away—it was too complicated.

So off we went, the three of us, into the thick cedar forest that spanned the mountains of the border between Canada and the United States.

I knew the road we'd been on from Polebridge crossed the border in a few miles, and though the crossing was closed, I knew it would have cameras and sensors, and there was no way we wanted to try to cross there.

It also made sense that there would be sensors and cameras along the border at places where people were likely to cross, so our best bet was to cross where least expected. To me, that meant out in the middle of nowhere, as far as possible from roads. Going straight north right through the thick woods would be our best way.

It suddenly struck me what an incongruous team we were—a giant hairy Bigfoot, a somewhat broken-down scraggly human, and a small scruffy dog.

I was pretty sure the Canadian Border Patrol had never seen the likes of us—and I hoped they never would.

I had no idea how far we still were from the border, but I guessed around five to ten miles from a map I'd seen in the Polebridge store. It would be a good hike in any case. I reluctantly led the way.

The going was slow, and I seemed to be the limiting factor. I knew Hap could make really fast time, and Wagger seemed able to run along just fine behind him.

That I was slow and out of shape became more and more apparent as we dragged along, slowly making our way through the thick timber.

I could tell from the sun that it was now mid-afternoon. Nothing had changed all day, we just trudged along, stopping a few times for snacks and water.

I wondered how Hap was doing staying awake, as I knew he was a nocturnal animal, and being awake all day would be to him like me staying up all night. But he seemed OK.

The day wore on, and it was soon feeling like time to stop and make camp, though there wasn't much to do, just spread out some cedar boughs and put my bag on them.

But the sun was beginning to fade, and I wanted to find enough wood to make a fire, one that would burn all night if need be. I no longer had the safety of the van, a fact that was foremost in my mind, now that we were in this wild forest.

It's hard to gauge how far you've walked when you're constantly going around trees and up and down drainages, but I was pretty sure we had to be in Canada at that point.

I had tried to keep a sharp eye out for cameras, but hadn't seen anything. We hadn't been on anything but animal trails, so I seriously doubted if this was a prime place for illegals to cross.

I stopped to look around for a good spot for my bed when I first heard it, and I had to stop and really strain to be sure my ears weren't playing tricks on me.

It sounded like something coming, but I wasn't sure what it could be, but it was kind of a mechanical sound, not like an animal. I picked up Wagger.

The sound got louder, but it seemed to have an inconsistency to it, like something turning and going back, then coming forward again.

Just as my brain formed an image and I realized what it was, it was too late—the chopper was coming fast towards us, very low, just above the trees.

I dove to the ground, but I knew it was hopeless. We were in a bit of a clearing and there was no cover.

I hit hard, Wagger still under my arm, fully prepared to hear the chopper stop and hover over me.

I could then hear Hap casting, "Make yourself into a ball and don't move."

Next thing I knew, Hap was on top of me, his legs and arms bunched up over mine, as if trying to hide me.

But I knew it was useless—if they saw Hap, they would stop, whether they saw me or not, for it's not every day one sees a Bigfoot, even in the wilds of Canada.

CHAPTER 31

Sure enough, the chopper was now hovering right above us, and it occurred to me that they might decide to shoot. If they realized they were looking at a Bigfoot, it would be the find of the century—no, the millennium.

I lay still, barely able to breathe with the weight on me, but I do recall thinking Hap wasn't as heavy as he looked. It was kind of like having a football player fall on you, not a huge Bigfoot.

I later thought about this, and it confirmed my other observations about Hap's size, adding more puzzlement to the theory of what he was made of.

The chopper hovered above us for what seemed like forever. Before long, Wagger started wiggling, trying to get away, but I managed to hold onto him.

Finally, the chopper moved on.

I couldn't believe it. I realized I'd been unable to breathe more from fear than from Hap's weight.

"Stay down," Hap cast. "In case flying stinger comes back."

"Flying stinger?" I asked, then laughed with relief. To Hap, a helicopter looked like a huge flying insect with a big long stinger. It seemed comical.

I knew it had been the border patrol, and I wondered if they thought Hap was a dead bear—a really big dead bear. It would make sense, since he was face-down and all they could see was his dark brown color and size—assuming they could see him at all. Maybe all they'd seen was a blur, a blobsquatch.

"Hap, let's go. We don't want to be here if they come back. Who knows, they might decide to make sure you're really dead, use you for target practice."

"Hap never thought of that," he cast, a bit disturbed, jumping up.

We took off for cover in the trees, but the chopper never came back. I hid for a good hour until it was nearly dark, then I gathered a few boughs and made myself a bed.

It was still light enough to gather some firewood, so I did, then sat down and split a can of beef stew with Wagger, more and more irritated that Hap had eaten all the huckleberry goodies.

Hap was long gone, and I was again feeling a bit spooked by being alone in the deep forest. I managed to gather enough wood for a fire and soon had one going.

I sat on a rock, watching the embers pop and the smoke twist into the air. Wagger lay at my feet, and I listened to the night sounds—crickets and what sounded like a loon far in the distance, followed by the sound of an owl.

I felt lonely and lost, but what was new? I wondered what Hap was doing and where he was—probably off foraging or whatever he did for food.

But then my thoughts went to Tracker. I felt a black cloud descend over me, and for some reason, it seemed like he could be near. I threw more wood on the fire, making it bigger, and moved a bit closer to the makeshift fire ring I'd built from rocks.

Now the owl and loon were calling again, but this time they both seemed closer, and from the direction of the loon I could now hear what sounded like someone hitting a tree with a baseball bat.

Wood knocking! There had to be other Bigfoot here besides Hap, and they were communicating. The owl and loon were classic Bigfoot imitations, from what I'd heard, and they were getting closer.

And now I could hear what sounded like a baby crying out in the woods, and I knew that was another Bigfoot trick.

I pulled my pack closer to me. What if they'd heard I was carrying the Book of Runes and were coming for it? Maybe the trio up at Blacktail had spread the word.

I felt the small Glock in my pocket, then smiled wryly. No way would the gun have even a small impact on a Bigfoot, not unless I could shoot it in a very strategic place, and the only way I would do that was if I were attacked. But if they wanted the book that bad, they could have it.

Now Wagger was growling at something I couldn't see, and a small rock was thrown into the fire ring, barely missing me.

I jumped up, startled and scared. I'd heard of this behavior, but never experienced it. Hap was the first Bigfoot I'd ever been around, and where the hell was he when I needed him?

Now a small tree branch came whizzing in, once again barely missing me, landing in the fire, spraying sparks all over. I quickly stomped them out. The last thing I wanted was a forest fire.

A scream now cut through the air, so loud it nearly knocked me down, or at least felt like it. It was high-pitched like a mountain lion's scream, but much more primal feeling, more sentient, like some creature who could easily outsmart me and was trying to terrify me—and its tactics were working.

I grabbed Wagger, who was trying to climb my leg and get into my arms for safety.

And now, seeing how scared Wagger was, I got mad. Who the hell did this Bigfoot—and I knew then it was a Bigfoot—think it was, to come into my camp and try to scare me? Even if I were in its territory, I wasn't doing any harm and wouldn't be staying long.

I looked straight in its direction and cast, "I don't know who you are or why you're so angry, but you'd better be forewarned—I'm Packy, Bearer of the Book of Runes, and I don't like your attitude. You might want to tone it down a bit."

All was quiet, and I knew I had cast my thoughts to it successfully. I sensed surprise, hesitation, almost fear.

I added, "Come and sit by the fire with me and tell me about your country here. I have a mission on behalf of your kind, and I need your help."

I didn't expect anything and actually just hoped they would go away, but I was soon shocked to see not one, but two giant Bigfoot slowly walk from the shadows towards where I stood, their eyes glowing red in the blackness of the thick night.

CHAPTER 32

"Who are you?" I cast.

"Gwa'wina, Raven," answered one, then the other said, "Hamumu, Butterfly."

"I'm Packy, Bearer of the Pack," I said, nodding towards them. "This is Wagger, He Who Wags When Not Scared to Death."

Wagger had his head stuffed under my armpit, trying to hide.

I continued, "Sit down. I have many questions, and you can ask me some, too, if you want."

The two Bigfoot sat down on their huge haunches, but not too close to the fire. They seemed leery of it.

"What kind of names do you have?" I cast. "It seems all you Bigfoot have strange names, and they usually translate to something in nature."

Gwa'wina answered, "Kwakiutl names, from the old people who were here long ago. They gave us our names."

"Are you that old that the original natives named you?" I asked.

"No, but we have names that signify our origin. They're passed to us through our families."

"What do you mean by origin?" I asked.

147

"Where we were born. We are from here, but many are not. Since most range, it helps us to know where they came from."

"Have you heard of Takoda?"

"Yes, everyone knows who Takoda is."

"Why is he so famous?"

"His Greats brought us the Book of Runes. You claim to be its bearer. We don't normally have anything to do with humans, but if you bear the book, we need to know where you are taking it and why."

So far, Gwa'wina had done all the talking while Hamumu sat silent. It appeared to me that Hamumu was a female, even though she didn't remind me too much of a butterfly. At least her friend was black, like a raven, but she was reddish black, not like any butterfly I'd ever seen.

I asked her, "Where is Takoda from, his name?"

She cast, "He is Lakota."

"How can a Bigfoot be a Native American?"

"Don't know Native American," she replied.

I sighed. "How can a Bigfoot be Lakota?"

"He's from that region. Before we were given the Book of Runes, long ago, Bigfoot helped the humans. They lived in peace with them, taught them our lore and they taught us theirs. They taught us naming, how it's good to have names."

"How do you know this?" I cast. "Wasn't it long long ago, way before your time?"

Now Gwa'wina answered, "She's a storyteller—one of those who carry our stories. It's a talent few have, to be able to remember. But why are you, a human, carrying our sacred book? Where is it?"

"Would you like to see it?"

Now both Bigfoot stood, as if to flee.

Gwa'wina cast, "We will die. It's defacing the sacred for us to see it."

"Then why can I carry it and still live? I'm nothing special."

"Who gave it to you?"

"No one. I took it, but with Takoda's permission, kind of."

"And you're still alive? Why are you carrying it?"

"I'm taking it somewhere."

This seemed pretty vague to me, but they didn't question it.

"Look," I continued, you really should see it. It's a once in a lifetime opportunity. You can tell your grandkids you held the Book of Runes."

With that, I pulled the book from my pack. Now both Bigfoot stepped back, as if they were going to be struck or something. I wondered if I myself had a death wish, to be so free with their supposedly sacred book, but I was beginning to have a mission, to free them of their superstitions, superstitions that I suspected had been born with the Book of Runes.

I opened the book to the pictures of the two crowned Bigfoot.

"Aren't they a lovely couple?" I cast, a bit sarcastically, though they didn't seem to notice.

Both came near to see, but not near enough to touch the book.

Hamumu answered, "It's Takoda's Greats."

149

"Yes, they were trying to help with the book. But it's flawed. I was chosen to return it to wherever—I don't know yet—but basically to get rid of it."

Both Bigfoot looked shocked. I suspected that if they weren't afraid of being struck by lightning, they would've grabbed it from me, then maybe throttled me.

"Look," I continued. "It was created by a human, Erik the Red. He was a bloody Viking."

"Hamumu don't know bloody Viking," she said, pausing for a moment, then continued, "Wait. Viking...very old, long ago, from across the sea, humans with red hair, blue eyes, yes, my Greats talked about them, too."

"They were just humans, like me," I cast. "Nothing special. The Red, he helped Takoda's Greats make this book. He was trying to help your kind, but it's been very bad for you. Time to get rid of it, get a new paradigm, one without all the bullcrap."

"Hamumu don't know bullcrap," she cast, frowning.

I laughed. "Good. Your kind are honest and good. Erik the Red was wrong. Tell everyone you meet the Book of Runes is history and they should go back to the old ways. Tell the stories of the old ways, the natural ways, before the Book of Runes came along. It's important."

"What does the book say that's so wrong?" asked Gwa'wina.

"I don't actually know," I replied. "I can't read runes. Except stuff about how fire's good and how you shouldn't befriend humans—ironic as hell, coming from a human. But Takoda is nearby, he will tell you."

I had sensed Hap in the bushes, watching.

"Takoda is here?" asked Gwa'wina, just as Hap stepped out of the forest.

"Takoda is here," Hap answered, holding out his arm to Hamumu. "I hold your arm with good feelings in my heart."

Hamumu and Hap shook arms as did Gwa'wina, who then turned and said, "Takoda, Otaktay is not far away. He's telling everyone you're a traitor and should be killed. Is this true?"

Hap frowned, then answered, "Otaktay wants the Book of Runes for some reason I don't understand, but it has to do with humans. He's not to be trusted."

We all stood there by the fire in silence. I wondered if the couple believed us or Tracker.

"Where is he?" I finally asked.

"He is nearby," cast Hamumu. "But he won't come with the fire here. He's deathly afraid of fire, ever since he burned down the forest and his child died."

I groaned. Not another tale where the once-good guy is destroyed by some tragedy that makes him bitter and evil. Like the sacred, I didn't do archetypes or stereotypes or whatever that would be.

"Tell Tracker to come on in and we'll talk," I said, surprising myself. "Tell him Packy has the book he wants, but Tracker ain't gonna get it because I know he wants it for nefarious purposes. And yes, I know you don't know nefarious purposes—the only reason I do is I used to read detective novels."

The two stood there, swaying a bit, and I knew they didn't understand and were nervous.

Finally, Hamumu cast, "We will tell him, but he's no friend of ours. We will pass by his nest, though."

As the couple turned to go I added, "And tell him I hope his leg is better and he's recovered from his accident, because we have a long grueling journey ahead."

CHAPTER 33

I was thinking about what the couple had said about Tracker being afraid of fire as I built the fire up a bit more. Hap stood watching.

"You're not afraid of Tracker?" he cast.

"Why should I be afraid of a coward?" I cast back.

"Tracker's a known traitor. He's the one working with humans to betray his own kind."

"Why would he do that?"

"Because he's bitter about his role in killing his child," I replied, "Or supposedly. That's probably the rumor he's spreading around. I think he's simply selling out."

I said it in unison with Hap, "Hap don't know selling out."

"Look," I continued. "Tracker's being ferried around by a human or maybe humans. Why would a human ferry a Bigfoot around?"

"Hap don't know. Maybe they're trying to get the book."

"Way back at the cave, when I was stealing the book, you told me they'd put Tracker on our trail. Who was this they?"

"Those who disagreed with getting rid of the book."

"Who exactly are they?"

"They are the ones who have the most to lose."

"And who is that, exactly?"

"The ones who teach the book. The Teachers."

"The Teachers? You mean to tell me there are Bigfoot who actually teach what's in the book? I guess that makes sense. Teacher rhymes with preacher. And don't ask, I'm not in the mood to tell you about preachers."

Hap was silent, now sitting a ways from the fire, Wagger by his side.

I cast, "So, Hap, Tracker was sent by the Teachers, but he's also working with humans. Very confusing."

Hap shook his head back and forth in agreement.

I continued, "I think Tracker is trying to get the book for the humans and he's been promised something for it. Something so enticing that he can't say no. He's lying, telling the Teachers he's working with them, but it's actually with humans. What would a Bigfoot find so enticing he would betray his own kind for?"

"Hap don't know," he cast, looking tired and dejected.

"You guys have pretty much everything. You browse for food. You build your own nests. What does a Bigfoot need?"

"Nothing."

"Well, Tracker's being influenced by a promise of something. Free food forever?"

"Hap don't know."

"If he were angry about losing his child to fire, well, the book preaches fire, so he'd be on our side, wanting to see the book destroyed, right?"

Hap was silent. He now appeared to be licking some kind of stick.

"What are you eating, Hap?"

"Honey stick."

I got up and walked over to take a closer look. The stick was covered with ants. Hap licked the ants off, then put the stick back into a nearby anthill, and when the stick was again covered with ants, he repeated the procedure.

"Is it good?"

I felt gaggy watching him, but I knew bears and other primates did the same thing.

"Yes," Hap replied. "Except they wiggle. But don't eat red ones, they're bad for you. All red insects bad." He then added, "Maybe Tracker wants pancakes."

"Bingo," I cast back. "I think you're right. They're promising him human food and comfort and safety for the rest of his life. Probably on some habituation farm in Arkansas or Tennessee somewhere where they can also get his DNA for proof. Except they're lying to him."

"He'll kill them if they are."

"Not if they kill him first."

"Why would they kill him?"

"Hap, most of my kind doesn't believe Bigfoot exists. The first person to bring in real scientific evidence, like a body, is going to be rich."

"Hap don't know rich."

"Sure you do, free food forever."

"Hap already rich."

"Yes, you're rich, but we humans have to work for our food. And no, I'm not in the mood to explain our economic system. Are you going foraging tonight with Tracker nearby?"

"No, just eat honey stick."

"Will you keep the fire going?"

Hap hesitated, then cast, "Hap don't like fire, but OK, for Packy and Wagger."

"Thanks, Hap," I cast, then got my sleeping bag, grabbed Wagger, and crawled down into it. I lay there for awhile and was almost asleep when Hap cast, "Packy, would you kill Hap for science and to be rich?"

"No, Hap, I would never do that. Hap's my friend. No amount of pancakes would ever let me feel good about killing a friend. I was in a war, Hap, and I didn't even feel good about seeing my enemies killed, yet alone my friends."

I saw Hap's teeth in the firelight. He was grinning.

"Hap watch over Wagger and Packy at night, and Packy watch over Hap by day."

"Friends," I replied.

"Friends," Hap cast in agreement.

"Even friends will lie to each other," a dark voice cast from beyond the firelight, a voice I instantly knew was Tracker's.

CHAPTER 34

"Otaktay, you are the only Bigfoot I know who understands lying," Hap cast back.

I quickly crawled out of my bag, Wagger in my arms, and stepped close to the fire. I felt fear, but yet I didn't—it's hard to explain.

Maybe I was feeling fear on behalf of Wagger and Hap, hoping nothing bad would happen to them, but I really didn't worry that much about myself.

That feeling gave me what some call courage, but I knew differently—when you don't care, you tend not to worry or be fearful, and that's not the same as caring but acting anyway, which is what real courage is. But sometimes, the outcome is the same, regardless, and that's what really matters, I guess.

Tracker now stepped from the trees and into the shadows cast by the fire, and I could tell he had a serious limp from the accident. I knew he wouldn't come any closer, as long as we had a fire going.

Since ditching the van, I was now keeping the pack with the book close to me and had put my Glock in its side pouch. I now reached in and surreptitiously pulled the gun out. Somehow, Tracker knew, as I saw him stand back a bit.

"Death flinger," he cast, with fear in his thoughts, then immediately stepped back into the trees, but I knew he was still nearby.

"Look, Tracker," I cast, "You're playing with fire again, just like when your child died."

Hap looked at me somewhat surprised, but I continued.

"The fire is set by humans this time, Tracker, and you're going to be the one who gets burned. The humans you're hanging with and trusting are Bigfoot researchers. I don't know how you hooked up with them or what they're telling you, but they want more than just the Book of Runes. After you give them the book, they'll kill you. They know they need you to get the book first, but then they get the Bigfoot. At that point, they'll have a valuable document and also a Bigfoot body, one that can't fight back. They'll be rich and famous. They plan to kill you Tracker, after you give them the book. Don't be naive."

Just then, a huge branch came lofting in, nearly hitting me, and right after that, a large rock, barely missing Hap. I quickly figured out that having a fire wasn't going to keep us as safe as I'd originally thought.

I now pulled out the Glock and shot in Tracker's direction, though not at him, aiming a bit high. I didn't want to injure him, just scare him. The shot echoed through the woods, splitting the quiet of the night. Wagger cowered under my arm.

"Now everyone knows where we are," Hap cast with concern.

"Seems to me they already knew," I cast back. "The fire pretty much told everyone. Besides, who's out here besides Tracker and the pair we met earlier?"

"Hap don't know. Now we'll find out."

157

All was quiet, not even a stick or stone from Tracker. I hoped the gunshot scared him off, but it didn't seem likely he would go very far.

I stood close to the fire, holding Wagger under my arm, ready to shoot again if necessary, but it felt like Tracker had left.

It was then that I first really noticed that I seemed to be developing a sixth sense about such things, one I now believe all humans once had and can maybe rekindle under the right conditions.

After all, animals seem to be aware of things in their environments that they can't necessarily see, so why not humans? We've all heard the stories of horses perking up their ears at things they can't see over a hill, although maybe they just have a keener sense of hearing.

But there are stories about animal behavior before earthquakes, which could be their sensitivity to infrasound that's caused by huge underground plates moving. There are lots of things we humans haven't yet figured out, and losing senses and things we no longer need when buffered by civilization could be among them.

As we waited, I kept the fire built up, but I was soon feeling the effects of the long hike. I was exhausted and needed to sleep.

I pulled my bag closer to the fire, crawled down into it with Wagger, my gun nearby, and was soon fast asleep— my last memory being of Hap shaking his head and casting frustration because all the ants had also gone to bed and his honey stick was failing him.

But it was all too soon that I felt Hap gently kicking my side with his big foot while casting in panic, "Get up, Packy, up!"

CHAPTER 35

As I struggled to wake up from a deep sleep, I could smell smoke from the fire, but it had taken on a more distinct smell—that of burning grasses.

I immediately knew something was wrong, and I was right. The fire had spread from the fire ring and was quickly igniting the nearby forest understory of dry leaves and shrubs.

"Quick, Hap!" I cast. "Help me put it out!" I ran to the edge of where the fire had spread, while Hap started kicking dirt onto the fire with his big feet. Wagger looked terrified, but stayed by my bedroll.

The fire had burned from the fire ring into some nearby grasses, then had climbed into a small pine and was quickly spreading. I tried to put it out, stomping and kicking dirt at it, but it had soon climbed into the tree beyond my reach. Hap couldn't do anything, either, as it was too hot.

The forest was dry, and the fire spread quickly. I knew we had no choice but to retreat, so I ran back and grabbed my pack, quickly tying my sleeping bag onto it.

Hap and I both stood there for a minute in shock and despair, as the fire jumped into a second tree, then a third. I had no idea which way we should retreat, as the fire seemed to be spreading in a circle, but Hap kept his cool a bit better and noted which way the breeze was blowing.

"We go now, Packy," he cast, leading me away from the flames. I grabbed Wagger and obediently followed, aghast at what we'd done. I knew what a forest fire would mean—death to many animals and maybe even to us.

We were still near the border, and all I could do was hope the border patrol would react quickly. But at the rate it was burning, a lot of damage might be done in the meantime.

I could see the first light of dawn to the east and knew we would soon be able to see better, but right then it was tough going because it was still dark. I couldn't see a damn thing and kept running into bushes.

After falling several times, I felt Hap's big arms helping me up, then lifting me and Wagger onto his shoulders.

With Hap's night vision, we were soon making good time, but it wasn't long until the smell of smoke became more distinct. I knew it was catching up to us, but there was nothing we could do.

Hap was now in a full-on run, and I was again amazed at how fast he could go, especially in the dark, where I couldn't see anything, and I could tell he was going uphill.

It seemed like Hap ran forever up through the thick timber. I knew we were near the top of the drainage when we finally came to a big boulder field, as the sun was now rising and I could begin to make things out.

Hap stopped to catch his breath, putting me and Wagger down. As he stood there huffing, I could make out the fire below us, and it had spread into a huge red mass that was quickly following us up the slope. A heavily treed area stood between us and the fire, and I knew when it hit the thicker trees, it would run uphill like a demon.

Hap needed to rest, but we also needed to get out as fast as we could. Fire travels in the direction of the breeze, which usually flows uphill, and in a fire, the hot breeze preheats the fuel in front of it, making everything burn even faster.

I knew that once we crested the hill, we could drop down the other side, where the fire would be slowed, as fire tends to go slower downhill.

I cast to Hap, "I know you're tired, but we need to go. The fire's catching up."

"Hap can't go now, Packy. Side hurts. Need more time. Go without Hap."

He was all bent over, still huffing and puffing.

"Are you going to be alright? Can you catch up to us?"

"Hap be OK. Hurry, go!"

Against my better judgment, I took Wagger and started towards the crest of the hill. I knew Hap could catch us in minutes, covering terrain that would take us a long time to hike. By us going ahead, it would give him a shorter distance with us on his back.

I knew not to run, as I would soon flag out, even though the pace of the fire made me want to flee as fast as I could. But I walked on up that hill at a steady pace, one that wouldn't leave me winded like Hap was. I carried Wagger, not wanting him to panic.

The hill was now steep enough that I had to switchback to get up it, flailing through tree branches and thick scrub. It seemed like for every step I would take, I'd slide backwards two. I could now hear the roaring of the fire clearly, and it wasn't that far behind.

As I struggled up that huge hill, I began to worry about Hap and wish he would catch up. I was feeling remiss for leaving him.

But I had no choice but to concentrate on myself, as every switchback was a test in my resolve. I was beginning to get winded on the steep slope, and I could hear the fire catching up to us. The roaring inferno was getting closer and closer, and all too quickly.

I have no idea how long or how far I hiked, as the terror I felt made all my senses collapse into a microcosm of nothing but a desire to survive. I was sure the fire had reached Hap, and I was beginning to feel sick, both physically and mentally—sick from smoke and exertion and sick from leaving my friend behind.

I finally crested the divide where I could look down a huge drainage to a long crystal blue lake far below. I estimated it to be a good two or three miles downhill.

I stood there in terror, the fire roaring like a dragon behind me.

Where the hell was Hap?

CHAPTER 36

I waited for a few minutes at the crest, trying to cast to Hap, but got no answer. Finally, I headed downhill, quickly making my way to another boulder field, where I sat and waited a bit, catching my breath.

I could no longer see the fire, but smoke billowed up and cut through the clear air like a knife through soft butter.

Where was Hap? I studied the crest above and saw nothing, except that the smoke seemed to be closer. It was time to go.

It was much easier going down the hill, even though we were in thick forest and I had to bushwhack to get through it. After about 15 minutes, I stopped and turned around to see what was going on.

The saddle I'd just crossed was engulfed in flames, some looking to be 50 or 60 feet tall. I just stood there, me and Wagger, watching it rage. I've never seen anything like it before, and I hope to never see anything like it again.

I was heartbroken by the fact that we'd started this—I could now add arson to my list of infractions. But I was also heartbroken knowing there was no way Hap could've survived.

I began the long slog down. I knew the lake would be my only real refuge.

As I trudged down, even Wagger seemed broken and tired, and I began wondering about the Book of Runes. How could I possibly ever take it to wherever it was supposed to go without Hap's help?

Especially now that I was in such primitive wild country—Bigfoot country, no less. And any Bigfoot worth his salt would take the book from me upon knowing about it, and I assumed all would soon know, given the notoriety I seemed to be getting.

Me and Wagger finally made it to the edge of the lake, where I got a drink, splashed water over my head, then sat against a tree, exhausted.

As I sat there, trying not to feel despair, I made out a small figure on the slope high above me, not far from where I'd come down, crossing a secondary ridge. At first I felt a thrill—it had to be Hap!

But then I felt a chill—I could tell from the size and limp that it was Tracker—but he was heading uphill, not coming after me, but headed straight for the fire. He obviously couldn't see where it was through the thick smoke. He had to be disoriented—maybe even have smoke inhalation.

I knew Tracker would kill me if he could catch me, yet I was overcome with pity for him, and pity can be a dangerous thing, both for its bearer and its receiver. I knew that, but I couldn't help myself—it's just who I am.

I now got up and stepped out from the shadows so I could see him more clearly, and after a moment, without thinking about it twice, I frantically cast to him, "Tracker, go downhill. You're heading straight for the fire. Turn around—there's a lake below you."

Now I watched as Tracker turned and paused, looking around in confusion, then suddenly began running down the big hill, leaving the secondary ridge behind just as the fire crested it and came over the top, roaring and burning everything where he had just been, huge pieces of burning debris floating through the air in the wind created by the flames.

I lost sight of Tracker halfway down where the trees became thicker, but I could tell he had veered over away from me, so I wasn't too worried. I knew he was headed for the safety of the lake. I would be a low priority for him at that point—probably all he was thinking about was his own survival.

But suddenly, with no warning, Tracker stood next to me! I remember wondering how he'd got there so fast and not knowing what to do to protect myself, as my gun was in the pack on my back. I instinctively grabbed Wagger and crouched down.

The immense Bigfoot stood above me, looking down to where I sat crouched with my arms folded around my head in the posture I'd learned for protection from bears.

I tensed up, waiting for the first blow, but instead of attacking, the figure quietly cast, "Why did you help Otaktay?"

I looked up in surprise and answered, "I don't know. I guess because I'm stupid, Hap."

CHAPTER 37

Hap and Wagger and I stood by the lake, though I couldn't see much in the smoke, but the light that did come through made the waves look like glass.

From above, the lake had looked long and narrow, like so many glaciated lakes, like Bowman and Kitla behind us. I also knew if this lake was formed by glaciers, which it most likely was, it would be deep and scoured out and very cold.

Above us, the fire had slowed down and was moving very slowly towards us, but I worried that it would soon be on us.

"What should we do now, Hap?" I cast, tired and wanting nothing more than to eat and rest. I'd given Wagger a can of sardines, the last of any real provisions I had, unless one counts a few slices of bread.

"Walk around or swim," Hap replied.

I groaned. I already knew that. "I can't swim that, Hap. I'll die in about 10 minutes from hypothermia."

"Packy needs fur coat."

"Yeah, I know, like you have, but Packy only has skin. How long would it take you to swim it?"

"Not long."

"Could you do it without freezing?"

"Hap has thick hair."

"Could you swim it with me and Wagger on your back?"

"Not a problem."

"But how long would it take, Hap? Would I freeze to death in the meantime?"

"Long enough to get cold, Packy."

"Why don't we just walk around it?"

"Lake too long. The fire soon be here."

"And Tracker's out there somewhere," I added grimly. "OK, let's go for a little swim. You can swim, can't you, Hap?"

"Hap good swimmer."

"Can you swim fast?"

"Hap can swim."

I took the Book of Runes from my pack, along with what was left of the loaf of bread I'd bought in Polebridge. I emptied the plastic bread wrapper and carefully wrapped it tightly around the book, then stuck it down the front of my shirt.

I stuffed my sleeping bag into the pack, then secured it onto my back, grabbed Wagger under one arm, and was soon on Hap's shoulders.

As he waded out into the cold water, I grit my teeth, knowing what was to come would be far from a pleasant swim. It might even kill me, but what choice did I have?

And it did almost kill me, but not in the way I had expected.

I found out later that the lake was aptly named Frozen Lake, and it set right on the border. We had gone south a bit in our panic, and then turned back north, resulting in us crossing the border twice.

Once Hap was in the water deep enough to swim, I felt like there was no way we were going to cross that lake. The water was beyond cold—it was frigid, and once Hap was in, it came up around me almost to my shoulders. I knew I wouldn't last long. Funny, though, I wasn't worried about me, but rather about Hap and Wagger.

"Cold, Packy?"

"I don't think I'll last long, Hap. Will you take good care of Wagger?"

I wished now Hap had left the little dog with the older folks back near Polebridge, as it would be far superior than him trying to survive with me gone.

"Hap swim fast."

With that, he began swimming like I've never seen before or since. The immense power of his muscles thrust us through the water almost as if we'd been on a motorboat. I could barely hold onto him as he swam, his shoulders moving back and forth as he literally heaved us forward.

We were soon halfway across the big lake, but not soon enough. Just in the ten or so minutes it had taken us, I could feel my feet and legs going numb. My hands were in a bit better shape, as they weren't completely under the water, but they were also starting to feel extremely cold.

I knew it wouldn't be much longer before I would lose my hold. I had Wagger tucked under my arm, and I worried about him, though he seemed to be staying somewhat dry.

"Packy getting colder, Hap."

"Hang on. Almost there."

But it was no use, I was beginning to lose the feeling in my hands. I held on for all I was worth. If I went underwater, there was nothing to save me, as I knew I couldn't swim in my condition.

It was then that a blackness came over me, a blackness that felt like being in the pits of war, a place I'd been and never wanted to go to again. I tried to push it from my mind but couldn't.

"Hap, Tracker's here."

I had no more cast the thought to Hap when I felt a huge hand grab my leg, pulling me off Hap's back and into the dark icy water, where I quickly went under.

It was only a moment before I blacked out and knew no more.

CHAPTER 38

I awoke coughing, my chest heavy with what felt like water. It was hard to breathe, but I knew I was somehow by a fire and safe.

My clothes were soaked and cold, and I felt panicky, wanting to get them off me. They felt heavy, like some great burden, and I knew they were keeping me from warming up.

I tried to get up, but my legs wouldn't move. They felt cold and hard to the touch, and my fingers didn't feel much warmer.

"Packy stay by fire," came Hap's cast.

I managed to sit up and look around. I had to be hallucinating. I was next to a cozy fire that burned in a stone fireplace made of the same kind of stone that Tracker had thrown at me what seemed like years ago by a different fire, the fire that had gone astray and lit up the whole forest.

I looked around more, and the fire cast shadows in what appeared to be an old log cabin. It had only one room with not much in way of furnishings, just a cast-iron cookstove and a bedspring with no mattress, which Hap was sitting on, his huge body making the springs sag almost to the floor.

I suspected we were in a border patrol cabin.

I tried again to stand. I had to get these wet clothes off. Even though I was right next to the fire, I was shivering. But then a fear filled me.

"Hap, where's Wagger?"

Wagger heard his name and came and sat by me, licking my face. He'd been by the fire also. I was relieved beyond words and just sat there, petting his cold nose, holding him close to me. Like me, he was soaking wet, though he seemed to be drying off much better.

"Hap, I have to get out of these wet clothes. Please help."

I could almost hear the bedspring sigh with relief as Hap stood. He came over and gently helped me pull off my Free Tibet shirt. I then managed to wiggle out of my jeans and crawl back over next to the fire, where I immediately started to warm up.

"What happened?" I cast. "Where are we?"

"Box by lake, Packy."

"You broke in? How did you start the fire?"

"All Bigfoot know how to start fire, Packy. We're taught that from the Book of Runes. And I know how to do it inside firebox from looking through windows, watching humans start fire."

"Just like your mom, eh, Hap, over in Weber?" I tried to tease, but my voice came out flat.

"Yes, Bigfoot like to look through windows. Humans interesting."

"Peeping Bigfoot, huh? Well, I'm glad you know how to build a fire cause you're saving my life with this one. What happened, anyway?"

"You slide off my back, Packy, so I reach back and grab you, but have big tug of war with Tracker, but Wagger bit him. Take you to the shore but you asleep from the water."

I couldn't believe it. Wagger bit Tracker? And lived to tell about it? Wagger had saved my life, even after all the times I'd tried to find him a new home. I felt very humble.

Hap continued, "Packy, Tracker got your pack and the book. I have to leave, go find him."

With that, Hap turned towards the door.

I cast, "I'm sorry, Hap. I failed you."

"It's OK, Packy, you did your best. Hap find Tracker, then come back."

I felt a surge of fear. What if Tracker killed Hap? Or what if Tracker came for me while Hap was gone?

"Hap, I dunno, maybe you should stay here. Forget the book. Too dangerous."

"Can't, Packy. You know that. Packy be OK?"

"I'll be OK, but I worry about you."

"Hap be OK. But Packy, what is this?"

Hap held up something wrapped in plastic. It was dripping and appeared to be soaking wet.

It took me a minute to figure it out, but I soon started laughing with relief. Hap just stood there, holding the dripping object, puzzled.

"Where'd you get it, Hap?"

"In your shirt," he answered.

"Open it, my friend."

Hap tried to open the package, but his big hands wouldn't cooperate, so he handed it to me. I unwrapped it and held up a perfectly dry Book of Runes.

It was the first time I ever heard a Bigfoot laugh, and it was worth all the pain and hardship and life-threatening events to hear.

It sounded like a babbling brook, like sitting in a wonderful cool forest glade on a sunny summer day with nary a care in the world, like how it felt when you were young with no idea at all of how cruel the world could be.

It was a sound of innocence and of delight and how you must feel when your dreams come true, all that wrapped up together.

His laugh filled the cabin and swept around me like an indescribable warmth, and I soon fell into a deep refreshing sleep, one that probably saved my life, if I only knew.

When I awoke it was early morning, the fireplace was cold, and my dry clothes were by my side, Wagger curled up asleep on them. Hap was gone, but I somehow knew he was fine and would soon return from his foraging.

I stood and got dressed, though my lungs still felt like lead, then walked to the nearest window to see where we were.

A short dirt airstrip was nearby, and I realized it was for bush planes. The lake sat a few hundred yards away, and smoke tendrils drifted across it, but it looked like the fire hadn't yet made it to this side.

I hoped the lake would be a big enough barrier, but I also knew that spot fires were often started by floating debris, allowing a fire to get around natural barriers.

I was hungry, so I'd started going through the cabin's cupboards when Hap came in and announced he wanted pancakes. I just stood there and laughed.

I was so happy to be alive, so happy Wagger and Hap were alive, and so happy that we still had the Book of Runes that I felt giddy.

What I later realized was that my giddiness wasn't from happiness, but was my body trying to tell me I was very sick.

It was the beginning of an illness that would take me as close to death, if not closer, than Tracker had done when he pulled me underwater—an illness that would also reveal the secret of the maps in the Book of Runes and thereby set us on our rightful course, if I could survive long enough to follow it.

CHAPTER 39

I knew we had to be in a patrol cabin by the way the cupboards were stocked, as they were crammed full of canned goods and such.

I had found some pancake mix and was about to get started cooking when Hap came up to me, choking and gasping. I noticed he had a can of Folger's coffee in his hand. He'd obviously sampled the grounds, which were all over his chin.

"Spit it out, Hap," I cast as he started doing just that. Soon there were grounds all over the cabin floor. It looked like he'd managed to sample about half of the five-pound can.

"Jeez, Hap, what a mess! It's bad enough we're using the cabin without permission, we don't need to trash it out."

"What is it?" he asked.

"Coffee. Give me that can, I need a cup."

I found a pan and sent Hap to the lake to fill it with water. He was soon back, and I put the pan on the stove and poured in some grounds. Hap then handed me two large cutthroat trout, which he must've caught while getting the water.

"You going to eat these, Hap?" I cast, wondering if he'd changed his mind about eating meat.

"No, for Packy and Wagger."

"Thanks," I cast, well aware of how much he hated to kill anything. He must've known we were hungry for protein.

Hap then told me that he had stolen them from a grizzly bear, and I had to laugh, especially when he said the grizz was too scared of him to argue. Of course, I found out much later that this was a wild story Hap had invented so I wouldn't know he was killing fish on my behalf.

Hap then began going through the cupboards, and I decided it would be a good idea to confiscate some of the canned goods for our journey.

When the coffee began to boil, I slipped it off the stove and let it sit for a minute so the grounds would settle, then poured some into a cup, which I'd found in the cupboard.

"You want some coffee, Hap?"

He made a face which I took to mean no. He was trying to open a can of berries, so I got a can opener and tried to show him how to use it, but his hands were too big, so I opened the can for him. He basically drank it down in one gulp, then started rummaging through the cupboards again.

Since Tracker had taken my pack, I searched around the cabin and found an old green daypack and decided to fill it with food. As I was busy doing this, as well as drinking my coffee, a thought occurred to me.

Tracker had managed to pull my pack off my back, which I hadn't thought much of until now, as about all that was in there was my sleeping bag and some canned food—

but I had just remembered something else that was in there—my Glock.

I froze, terrified at the thought of Tracker having a gun. Even though it had gotten wet, it would probably still work.

"Hap, Tracker has my death flinger."

Hap froze.

I asked, "Will he figure out how to use it?"

"Hap don't know."

"Oh man, now what?"

Hap looked very concerned.

I had no idea where Tracker was, but I suspected he wasn't that far away. I started putting food in the pack and forgot about making pancakes. I was starting to feel chilled again, disoriented, and not thinking clearly.

But I knew we were being stupid by relaxing. We needed to get out of the cabin and get back on course. And I'd somehow forgotten about the fire outside—who knew how close it was by now? Just because we couldn't see it from the window didn't mean it was out. Just then, Wagger started whining.

"Hap, we need to get going."

I stuffed the book down the front of my shirt again, then found a warm coat and down vest in a closet and stuffed both into the pack. What I really needed now was another sleeping bag, but no such luck.

I found a bunch of beef jerky in a pantry and crammed all of it into the pack after giving some to Wagger. I then took an old army-style canteen from a nail on the wall.

I was feeling panicky, and I realized I was beginning to get hot, like a fever coming on. I couldn't get sick—this was the worst possible time. I forced myself to sit down and assess things.

I sat there for a minute, trying to collect myself. Hap was standing by the window as if watching something, and I soon realized what it was when the sound came closer.

A chopper! Was it the border patrol again?

"Packy, we go now," Hap cast, picking up Wagger, who'd been eating the jerky I'd given him and now had a big piece sticking out of his mouth like a cigar as he hung over Hap's big shoulder.

I went to the window. Sure enough, a chopper was coming, but it had a big bucket hanging from it on a thick cable. It flew to the lake and dipped the bucket, filling it, then turned and left.

"Firefighters, Hap. They're not after us. I'm wondering if the fire's jumped the lake yet."

I watched as the chopper turned and crossed the lake, then headed up the ridge we had come down the previous afternoon. I knew it was time to go, as the cabin would probably become a central point for firefighters.

"Let's go, Hap," I cast, opening the cabin door and looking up at the huge ridge before us, much bigger than the one we'd just crossed. I somehow knew that ridge led to an even bigger mountain, one we couldn't scale, so I instead turned west.

We would have to walk along the edge of the lake until we could see out more, but there was no way we were climbing that ridge, especially in the shape I was in.

We took off, Hap carrying Wagger, and me carrying the pack filled with canned goods and the canteen. We skirted the lake for what seemed like forever, walking through bogs and thick willows when not carefully traversing the bottoms of avalanche chutes that fell into the lake from the steep ridge above.

It was slow going, and the entire time I worried about Tracker, and I jumped every time we spooked a moose or deer. We stayed under that ridge for a long time, until it finally turned and started going north again. At that point, we were also at the end of the lake.

What I didn't realize was that we were skirting the huge massif that held Inverted Peak and Outlier Ridge, walking through the only drainage in our area that threaded through the Canadian Rockies, the only route that could be traversed without climbing huge ridges and peaks. We were leaving the Flathead River behind.

It was a fortuitous route, though we didn't know it at the time, as it put us on the right side of the mountains for our destination, as well as back closer to human habitation, which would be our only real protection from Tracker.

What I also didn't know was that we were once again back in the United States and would soon cross the border for a third time, again undetected. In fact, when later looking at a map, I figured our camp that night was right on the border.

By the time it was dark, I was again exhausted, and Hap had to gather all the firewood while I sat on a log and shared a can of beans with Wagger.

Hap brought the wood, more in one armload than I could've collected in ten, and he then left to go forage. I built a big fire and settled me and Wagger in as close to it as I dared, quickly drifting into a deep sleep, even though it was only evening and the sun was still casting a hazy red glow over the trees from the nearby forest fire.

And as I drifted off, I tossed and turned, wondering if Tracker would figure out how to use the gun. And I also wondered how Hap would react if he ever found out I'd used several pages from the Book of Runes as firestarter.

I was sick, but I really didn't understand that yet, and I began dreaming, dreaming that the moon had risen and I could see far into the distance, with the wildlands stretching far away in the moonlight.

And I dreamt of the woman I loved and who had divorced me when I came back from the war. I dreamt that Amy was standing there above me smiling, and I dreamt of our good times and of all she meant to me, until I woke in the middle of the night with the moonlight shining through the trees.

I thought I'd heard gunshots far far away, but then decided I'd been dreaming.

I just lay there and listened while Hap, who'd come back, snored, sleeping the sleep of the innocent, then I finally fell back to dreaming.

CHAPTER 40

"Packy, did you think Tracker would be your friend after you saved him? Instead, he tried to kill you."

"Hap, I don't trust anyone on this planet except maybe you. I didn't save Tracker's life because I thought it would make him a good guy. I'm not naive. I saved him because that's who I am. I would never just stand there and let someone die."

We were trudging along a stream that I later found out was called the Wigwam River. It had the classic braiding of a glacial stream and the pale-blue color that indicated it was carrying finely ground glacial till.

We had turned north again and crossed the Canadian border with nary a hint of trouble. The wide river valley was flanked by mountain massifs that had spring snow on their high ramparts.

A dirt road paralleled the river, but we stayed on the opposite side, making our way through the willows to avoid being seen, though there was no traffic.

Wagger was having fun, going into the river just enough to get wet, then coming back and shaking all over us. I was by now very attached to the little guy, and his acting like a puppy made me feel better, though it had been a tough day so far for me.

I seemed to have no energy, even though Hap had brought me two whitefish from the river for lunch. I knew he was worried about me. He had even built a small fire so I could cook them, and I knew he really didn't like messing around with fire.

As we continued, I started singing in time as we marched along.

"Row row row your boat, gently down the stream, merrily, merrily, merrily, merrily, life is but a dream."

"Packy OK?" Hap asked with concern.

"I'm tired, Hap. Can we stop for awhile?"

"Packy face red."

Hap stopped, and I crumpled to the ground next to him, then bunched my pack up as a pillow and stretched out. We had been walking all day and had stopped only to cook the fish.

Normally, given the slow pace we were walking, I would've been fine, not even tired. But now I was exhausted and chilled, even though it was a beautiful warm day.

It was then, lying there on the ground, that I noticed some dark tendrils in the sky, far above the western horizon, and they were soon followed by lenticular clouds that looked like giant flying saucers. They looked like the leading edge of a big storm.

This was not in the plan, I thought. I needed to stay warm and dry. What would we use for shelter? I knew Hap's warm waterproof coat would protect him, but neither Wagger nor I had one like it, though we did have the coat and vest I'd taken from the cabin.

I don't know how long I slept there on the ground in the sun, but when I woke, it was almost dusk, and Hap was pacing back and forth.

"Packy, we go now."

I was disoriented and not even sure where I was, but I stood and followed Hap, who was now carrying Wagger. A gust of wind hit us, and I knew the storm was coming in.

"Hap, I need shelter. I'm sick. I need shelter from this storm."

"Yes, Packy, Hap know. We stop soon and I make shelter for Packy and Wagger. We go into trees."

Hap led us into the forest at the edge of the riverway, and it immediately felt dark and threatening. I thought of Tracker and my gun.

"Hap, it's too dark here and scary. Let's go back out by the river where we can see around us."

"Hap need wood to make shelter, Packy."

"But we need fire, Hap, in case Tracker finds us, and also to stay warm. We don't want to start another forest fire. We need to get back out."

I was now shivering, even though I knew it wasn't cold. I stood there, refusing to go any deeper into the forest. It felt too primal, too dark.

"Packy right. We go back."

Hap turned and walked back into the open valley, stopping by a big rock.

"Packy and Wagger stay here."

Now Hap was gone. The shadows were getting long, and the forest looked downright spooky. I grabbed up Wagger and held him close to me, then sat down and leaned against the big rock as another gust of wind hit.

Soon Hap was back, carrying a huge armload of wood for a fire. He left to get more wood, and I started a fire, using more pages from the Book of Runes. I banked the fire against the big rock, hoping that would keep it from getting out of control.

Now huddled by the fire, I started feeling a bit better. I knew it would be colder here by the river, but I wanted to be out in the open.

Hap returned, but this time he had an armload of large branches that still had the leaves on them. He began building a lean-to near the rock and the fire, something to block the wind. And soon his little structure even had a roof, laced together with smaller branches and then stuffed with leaves and twigs.

All on all, it looked pretty weatherproof. It was now almost dark, and I was amazed at his skill and how quickly he had built it. We could all sit in it and yet still be near enough to the fire to stay warm. He had piled enough wood nearby to easily get us through the night.

We now stretched out, and I put on the coat I'd taken from the patrol cabin. I wrapped Wagger in the down vest, which he seemed to love, judging by the way he snuggled down into it. I still had that damn song stuck in my mind, "Row, row, row your boat...life is but a dream..."

We sat in silence, and I felt a fever coming on, making me want to ditch the coat, but I knew I should keep it on.

I cast, "I can't explain it, Hap, but all of a sudden I miss civilization. All this vast emptiness. I long for people, music, all the things we humans have to make life easier. It's too harsh out here on the edge."

"Hap sorry, Packy."

"Thanks, Hap. I know this is home to you."

Just then, the wind picked up, blowing a large branch from a tree, nearly hitting the shelter.

Hap cast, "Packy, what causes the wind?"

"I don't know, Hap. Something to do with cold air mixing with hot air. See, hot air is lighter and it rises, so when cold air comes in, it pushes out the hot air and this becomes wind."

"Like the hot-air balloon?"

"Exactly. The air in the balloon is hotter, so it rises, taking the balloon up and away."

"So that's why winds bring storms, rain and snow?"

"Exactly," I answered as another big gust of wind hit, the large rock protecting us and the fire.

"Packy, what causes storms?"

I knew Hap was asking me something, but I couldn't answer, for I was drifting off, just like a boat on Frozen Lake, heading for a dark and mysterious distant shore where a tribe of Bigfoot stood, waiting, their arms reaching out for the Book of Runes.

But soon, a giant Bigfoot named Otaktay pushed them aside, trying desperately to get to me, but at the last minute the boat I was in turned and disappeared into a sheltering bank of fog—fog that was hot like steam.

CHAPTER 41

Me and Hap and Wagger made it through the night, though I woke and tossed and turned many times, alternating between chills and fever.

I thought it would rain, but it didn't, and instead the wind blew and moaned. It was incessant. It wouldn't let up, and there was nowhere we could hide from it, no refuge.

It bothered us day and night as we trudged on for two more days, then it stopped, making us think it was over, only to start again in the middle of the night.

Hap's long hair blew until it became stiff, and I became irritable as hell, sick and every step a chore, except when Hap was carrying me. And the wind just wouldn't stop.

It whistled through the trees, making them groan and creak, limbs swaying and falling, leaves shredded. At times it sounded like a pack of wolves, and Hap would crouch down holding a big stick, ready to fight, then realize what it was. Other times it shrieked and reminded me of a flock of Pterodactyls. Then it would roar like a freight train.

There was nothing we could do but carry on, strained and weary and on edge, the towering mountains with their sheer cliffs above, watching.

And through all this, I got sicker and sicker, until I finally thought I might be dying. I spent most of my time hallucinating, and Hap would do his best to keep me going.

I knew now that I had a pneumonia, and it was getting more and more difficult for me to sleep as I coughed constantly, trying to clear the phlegm from my lungs, which were burning.

We continued to work our way north, up the valley that had been carved by the Wigwam River, staying out of sight in the willows, eating fish Hap had caught, and finally, finishing off the last of the canned food, which had been primarily beans and corn.

But by the end of the third day of the incessant wind, it didn't matter to me if we had food or not, as I had stopped eating. I knew Hap would make sure Wagger was fed.

Now, not that far ahead loomed Soowa Mountain, and beyond it, Mt. Broadwood. Across the flanks of the latter mountain ran a stunningly sheer ridge that was called the China Wall, and I knew it would stop us from any further progress north.

We had to turn and go west, crossing a big ridge that was dotted with stands of larches turning green in the spring chill, a ridge I knew I could never climb in my now-weakened state. I could feel myself fading with each day. I later found out that the ridge was the eastern flank of the Galton Range.

And I knew we had to cross that ridge to reach civilization and my only hope—antibiotics. I knew there had to be a city on the other side of that ridge because I'd seen airplanes crossing it at a low altitude as if they were cruising to a nearby airport.

Hap noticed them also.

"What is it, Packy?" He nodded towards a plane high above.

"Airplane."

"Hap don't know airplane."

"It's like a car and a balloon stuck together, Hap, sort of, anyway."

"Humans in it?"

"Yup, crazy humans. Gets you places fast, not like walking."

Hap was now guiding us entirely by intuition, although he claimed he was beginning to remember landmarks from his childhood. I found that impossible to believe, and I'd completely given up by this time on ever having a route or even a destination.

All I knew was that Hap had decided the Book of Runes was supposed to be taken to a so-called gathering place for Bigfoot, a place that had historically been the center of the Bigfoot universe, the Place Where the Sun Lingers. He had no idea why it was such an important place, but suspected it had something to do with the Book of Runes.

He had been there as a child, was born there, and had some vague recollection of it. What stood out most in his mind, and what was now guiding us north, was some huge granite spire he thought had to be in that direction.

Since the Canadian Rockies are sedimentary rock, mostly shale and limestone and not granite, I doubted that such a spire even existed. But I began to dream of that spire when I had a fever, and it was disturbing in its severity and its terrifying slopes that plunged into thin air.

Our progress was getting slower and slower, and I finally could go no further. We stopped, and even though it was only mid-day, I crumpled into a light restless sleep, Wagger next to me.

I don't know how long I slept, but when I woke, I was chilled to the bone. I couldn't get warm, no matter how I tried. I held my hands under my armpits and had my coat wrapped tightly around me.

"Hap, I'm freezing. I need fire."

"Hap get wood," he offered.

He quickly gathered wood and placed it in front of me. I was now shivering, but I managed to get my firestarter flint from my pocket. I stripped some dry bark from the logs he'd brought, then placed it in a little pile with some small twigs.

I struck my flint and it sparked, but failed to catch. I was shaking so hard I couldn't make a go of it. I tried again. I wanted to use a page from the Book of Runes, but Hap sat nearby, watching.

After several tries, Hap took the flint from me and had it sparked in one try, his big hands nearly engulfing the small piece of metal. The twigs began to smoke, and he leaned over them, gently blowing, until a small flame jumped up and he had a small fire going.

He then carefully, one by one, placed small twigs into the fire until it grew, then added larger and larger pieces of wood until he finally had a good-sized fire going.

I sat as near it as I could without catching myself on fire. Hap saw that it needed more wood and soon brought several larger logs. The fire was now crackling and popping, and I could feel the warmth seeping in, warming my bones.

I felt like I'd been hypothermic and my senses had been dulled, but now I was able to think more clearly. I envied

Hap and his thick hair and fast metabolism. He never seemed to be cold.

Maybe what I needed was a Bigfoot coat, I mused, turning around so my backside would get warmed up, once my front was so hot I could barely stand it.

"Hap," I cast, "I need a Bigfoot coat."

Hap showed his teeth.

"Hap no help," he cast back.

"I could cut some of that long hair off your arms, you don't need it all," I tried to joke.

He held his arms up, the long black shiny hair draping off them.

"Why humans no have hair?" He cast.

"We used to, but we lost it all. Except on our heads. I guess we didn't need it after we figured out how to make fabric."

"How Packy know this?" Hap asked.

"Because we get goosebumps when we're scared or cold. It's the remnant hair follicles from when we had hair all over us. When mammals get scared, their hair stands on end so they look bigger and predators will be scared off. And same when they're cold, their hair puffs out to make them warmer. See, yours does that, Hap. I've noticed your hair puffing out when you're scared."

"Scare me," he cast, showing his teeth.

"I'm afraid there's not much I could do to scare you, Hap."

I was now nice and warm, and I didn't want to get cold like that again. I then started coughing, my lungs filled with phlegm.

Just talking to Hap had worn me out, and I fell to the ground and curled up next to the fire in a ball, hoping I could make it through the night.

And through all this, I wondered where Tracker was, why he hadn't taken advantage of my weakness to strike, and I thought again about the gunshots I had heard during the night.

CHAPTER 42

The storm finally hit around five the next morning, and I was literally jolted awake by a huge bolt of lightning, which must have been very close, as I saw it through my eyelids at the same time I heard it.

That was just the beginning. The storm was fierce and fast, with bolt after bolt hitting nearby, pounding the ground and leaving the smell of ozone in the air. The fire had gone out, and Wagger was huddled in my arms in his down vest, terrified.

I was also terrified, and I managed to scoot me and Wagger away from the cold fire ring and up into some thick brush under the trees. I had no idea where Hap was.

Each bolt lit the sky a deep purple, and I knew it was the end. There was just too much lightning, too close, to not get hit. At least we would die fast, I thought.

This went on and on for at least an hour, though it seemed longer, until finally the front edge of the storm had passed on through.

I could hear it for another hour, moving on up the valley, until the thunder was far in the distance. It was followed by some huge raindrops that didn't last long.

Now it was dawn, and the humidity was playing havoc with my lungs, making me cough again. I was hot and soaked as if I had a fever, yet part of it was humidity from the storm.

"Packy, where are you?" Hap cast.

"Over here, under the trees," I answered.

"Big sky fire," he cast.

"Scary," I cast back.

"What causes it?" Hap asked.

I was coughing too hard to answer at first, but I finally cast, "Nobody really knows, Hap."

There was no way I could explain electricity to him, yet alone lightning, and nobody really did know how it happened. But the big front that had been blowing in for days was now past, and it appeared the majority of it had gone north of us.

I watched as the sun rose over Mt. Broadwood in a stunning display of golds and reds. I remember thinking it might be the last sunrise I would ever see, but not really caring very much. That huge ridge to our west was too much, there was no way I could ever cross it.

Hap seemed to sense what I was thinking, as he came over and put his huge hand on my shoulder.

I cast, "Hap, I'm sick."

"No more anger or sadness, Packy."

I at first thought he was referring to himself, then I realized he meant me.

"I know, Hap. But my lungs hurt. I damaged them living outdoors in winter, I was homeless. I froze them or something, and now it feels like they're infected, like pneumonia."

"Hap don't know lungs or infected or pneumonia."

I thumped my chest while breathing in and out. "My lungs, Hap, what takes the air in and out of you." I then started coughing again.

Sometimes I wished he understood more, as everything seemed so hard to explain. I was sick and impatient. It was all I could do to keep going. My lungs were on fire, burning, and it made me weak. All I wanted to do was sleep.

In fact, I wondered if now wasn't time for the endless sleep, as I felt like I could very well be dying. I had no energy, and taking one step took the utmost in difficulty.

Hap picked me up and sat me under a big tree, then disappeared into the forest. I had no idea where he was going or if he was coming back. At this point, I was only a liability to his mission. I wasn't even sure if he understood that I was sick, dying sick.

I must have drifted off, and I had no idea how long he was gone, but now I felt him pick me up again, like a little child. I was nothing to him, nothing.

He soon sat me down in the dirt in the direct sun. It felt like he had dug it out so it was like a recliner—I was partially sitting up and yet leaning back so I could rest. It was soft and comfortable, and I felt freshly packed leaves beneath me. That's where he'd gone, to find a suitable place and make me comfortable so I could die.

I cast my appreciation to him, then closed my eyes. I figured he would be gone when I awoke, if I ever did. I slept.

But I was soon awake, and now I was boiling hot. Hap had made my recliner in the direct sun, and it beat down on me, making me sweat. I couldn't open my eyes, the sun was so direct.

I cast Hap that I needed help. Soon he was standing in front of me, blocking the sun.

"Hap," I cast, "I'm too hot. I have to get out of here and into the shade. Please help me, Hap."

"Sun heal you. Hap right here."

"I need water."

Hap handed me my canteen, which he'd filled with the coolest sweetest water I'd ever tasted—it almost tasted like peppermint. I drank and drank until I could hold no more, then drifted back either to sleep or unconsciousness.

I have no idea how long this went on—all I recall was being so hot I thought I'd died and gone to hell. My lungs burned and burned. And just when I could stand no more, there was Hap with my canteen. I tried to pour water over my head, but he grabbed the canteen and stopped me.

I then knew night had fallen, as the relentless sun was gone, and I could feel Hap's back pressed against my side and Wagger in my lap. It was Hap's way of guarding me, I knew.

That night, I felt better until what I guessed to be about midnight, then the burning returned. I moaned and tossed and couldn't sleep.

I felt Hap get up and leave. Night was his time, when he could see best, and I knew he had gone to find food. I tried not to moan or move, as I knew he wasn't there to guard me, and I would be easy prey if Tracker were around.

Hap wasn't gone long, and when he returned, he again had me drink from my canteen, but now the water was bitter. I knew he'd put something in it, perhaps some kind of medicinal plant.

I finally slept, waking at dawn and feeling a bit better. My lungs still ached, but the burning was gone.

Hap asked if I were hungry, but all I wanted was more water.

It wasn't long before I started to fail again, and I new this would be the day that either saw me cured or dead. I really didn't care which it was at that point. All I wanted was relief.

Again the sun burned down, and again Hap gave me the bitter water. About mid-afternoon, I could take no more. I was drenched with sweat.

When the fever broke for a moment, I called Hap over to tell him goodbye.

"Hap, thanks for everything, but now it's over."

"Can't leave, Packy. Must come back, my friend, be healed."

"I can't, Hap, there's nothing more I can do. I can barely breathe. Every movement burns and hurts, and I'm so weak."

Hap came over and sat by me, then turned and put his arms around me and very gently held me.

"Hap help sun," he cast, his big chest against mine.

I thought about this later, and I know from this and from other contact I had with him that Bigfoot must run a temperature much hotter than a human's. This means they have a faster metabolism and need more fuel for energy, which goes against all mammalian biology, as the larger an animal is, the slower their metabolism seems to be.

How it can be, I don't know, but Hap was hot to the touch, and his added body heat almost put me over the edge. I was on fire, as hot as if I'd stepped into a raging forest fire.

I could feel myself drifting in and out of consciousness, and I knew my time was almost over.

I wanted only to die, to be free of the pain.

CHAPTER 43

As my mind began to drift, I slipped into a land I've never been in before, neither before nor since. I don't know where it is, nor do I want to ever return. It was a place of mists and strange half-formed beings, a place I know can't really exist, but yet it felt real.

I was running, holding something tight under my arm, something that kept slipping away from me, and I would have to stop and push it back into place. It was heavy and bulky and burned all along my arm where I carried it, from my wrist to my elbow.

Something terrible was pursuing me, something that wanted what I carried and would gladly kill for it.

I would run for awhile, then my lungs would burn, my arm would burn, and I would have to stop and catch my breath. I was so weak that it was all I could do to hold onto this thing I carried and continue.

Finally, as I leaned against a large moss-covered tree, thinking I could go no further, it occurred to me to see what it was that I carried and that was burning me.

I looked down and could see the spine of a large book, a book made of chewed leaves turned into paper with a deerskin cover. It was the Book of Runes.

Now whatever was pursuing me was almost on me. I had to run, yet I could go no further. My lungs burned so hot I could barely breathe, and I knew I would soon be consumed by the fire.

The Book of Runes would burn with me, and Hap would no longer have this impossible mission. I felt happy about that, suddenly wondering where Hap was. I hadn't thought of him until just then, as he wasn't part of the dream.

I made one last effort and ran, but could soon go no further. I collapsed against a rock wall that cut through the forest, some kind of volcanic dike. As I slipped down, I was suddenly in a cave.

It was the cave in the Flattops, the cave where I'd found the Book of Runes, what seemed long long ago. I rolled to the side of the cave, hiding in a small alcove.

Just then, the thing chasing me entered the cave, and I could now see what it was. It was a tall thin man with red hair! And somehow, I knew it was Erik the Red, the one who had authored all this madness to begin with.

I began to tremble, hoping he could neither see me nor sense my fear.

But it was too late, the Red turned and looked directly at me with eyes that burned like my lungs, burned like the Book of Runes under my arm.

His eyes spoke all I needed to know—they were filled with danger and disdain and a hatred I'd never before known.

I tried to push myself against the wall of the alcove, making it harder for him to reach me, but it was no use. He easily reached in and wrenched the book from under my arm.

I was suddenly filled with dread, for I knew that if the Red took the book, we could never fulfill Hap's mission, and the Bigfoot Nation was doomed.

Erik the Red was tall and of fair complexion and looked very intelligent, but his pale blue eyes were filled with anger.

He spoke, "You are trying to undo everything I've done to help the Bigfoot Nation. It was a great gift I gave them."

"A gift of poison," I replied defiantly, my fear now gone. I slipped from the alcove and stood face to face with the Red.

"Who are you, and what are you trying to do?" He asked.

"I'm Packy. They have to return the book to complete the circle, that's all I know. You must help, you helped create the book, you must know the secret of the maps."

"Why do you say my work was poison?"

"I don't know. They want to be rid of it. You have to help. What's in the maps? How can we read them? We have to return the book."

The Red opened the book, then carefully tore each map from it. He handed me the three maps, then took the book, turned, and left the cave, taking the Book of Runes with him.

I held the maps to me, again burning. Then, as I left the cave, I defiantly held them to the sky. He may have taken the book, but I still had the maps.

As I stood there, in my dream, the earth turned and the sun broke through the ragged clouds, sending a shaft of brilliant light directly on my path. As I held the torn pages, one on top of the other, the secret of the maps was finally revealed.

I woke, and my fever had broken, just as if someone had flipped a switch. It was over.

Someone was standing over me. Was it Erik the Red?

I looked up, and it was Hap. I was no longer dreaming, hallucinating.

"Packy talk a lot," he cast.

Now I felt panicky. The maps were gone! They'd been right here, in my hand, but now they were gone!

"The maps, Hap, the maps, where are they?"

"In the book, Packy. You've been dreaming. Drink."

He held the canteen to my mouth. I drank long until it was empty.

Hap shook his head in approval. "More?"

"I'm hungry, Hap."

Hap put his big hand on my forehead. He seemed pleased.

"Hap have food here. Eat."

He handed me some sort of paste-like stuff formed into a ball.

I didn't know what it was, but it tasted like acorns. It was a little bitter and yet had a pleasant nutty taste. I was famished and ate it in several bites. Hap had refilled my canteen, and I drank again.

"Rest, Packy. Hap get more food."

"I'm OK for now, Hap. Listen, I think I can read the maps now. I had a vision, and I think I can read the maps. Hap, let's see if I can read them."

I was excited, though still very weak.

I took the book from underneath my shirt and slowly unwrapped it from the plastic bread wrapper.

"Hap, we have to tear the maps out of the book to read them."

Hap looked unhappy. "Can't deface the book."

"Hap, look, you tell me you aren't superstitious, yet you treat the book like something with supernatural qualities. It's just a book, Hap. We have to tear the maps out in order to read them."

Hap carefully took the book from me.

"Packy no deface the book."

He looked unhappy, holding the book close to his chest.

I cast, "Probably what Erik the Red intended. Brainwash everyone that the book's sacred so they'll never rip out the pages that tell where it came from and thereby where to get rid of it." I paused, then asked, "Why would he put the maps in there in the first place if he didn't expect someone to take them out and use them?"

I knew Hap didn't have any more of an answer than I did. I got up, then turned and slowly began walking up the big ridge that stood between me and civilization.

"Where's Packy going?" Hap cast in concern.

"I'm going home, Hap. I know how to read the maps, but if you won't let me, there's no point in going any further. I'm tired of wandering though the wilderness. I sure as hell ain't no holy man, and it doesn't suit me anymore."

Wagger stood for a moment as if not sure who to follow, but was soon at my heels. I knew Tracker was down the valley somewhere, but without the Book of Runes, I was probably of no interest to him any longer.

I had to somehow get over that ridge, then I would be back with my own kind—assuming I wasn't too weak to get there, which was a big assumption.

CHAPTER 44

I started up the thickly forested ridge, Wagger at my heels, but only made it about 10 steps before I had to sit down and rest.

I could see Hap below me, standing and watching, now holding the Book of Runes out away from him like it was full of electricity or something. I felt bad, leaving him like this, but I just couldn't deal with anything anymore.

I stood again to continue, and the next thing I remember was blackness and voices and something huge and white carrying me over its shoulder, and climbing, climbing forever, all through the long night, then Hap talking in a fog and saying something about leaving me where people would find me.

I had drifted in and out of consciousness for what seemed like hours, and now all was quiet. I was sitting on something hard while Wagger sat in my lap and licked my hands.

I opened my eyes, and I could see the first streaks of dawn breaking across a huge mountain on the other side of what seemed to be a deep valley.

I was sitting in a wooden chair, one of those Adirondack types, and I turned and could see I was on the front porch of a house. By the drive was a sign that had flowers hand-painted around the words, "Fernwood Bed and Breakfast."

Now I could hear Hap casting to me, "Packy, one of the White Ones came and helped us. The human who lives here will help. She saved one of the Whites. Guard the book. Hap be back in two or three days."

I was disoriented and weak, but I did manage to cast a thanks to Hap and tell him to be safe. I could hear his footsteps rustling through the tall dry grasses, and when he was almost gone from earshot, I cast one last thing.

"Hap, where's the book?"

"Packy have book."

"I'm going to figure out the maps. When you come back, we'll know where to go."

I was surprised when he cast back, "Good, Packy, good."

I touched my chest and sure enough, the book was stuffed down into my shirt. I felt a sense of relief, knowing Tracker would now leave Hap alone.

But that sense was quickly gone when I realized I would now again be Tracker bait.

I sat up straight, trying to be alert. Where the hell was I? Now that the light was better, I could see I was on the front porch of a very nice English-style cottage.

Just then, a woman opened the front door. I got up, nearly falling, light-headed and dizzy.

"Do you need a room?" She asked. She had long dark hair and was wearing jeans and a plaid shirt.

"Yes," I answered, "But I guess it depends on how much you charge. I need something inexpensive."

"Well, come on in, we're just making breakfast."

I stood, but I had to lean against the doorjamb to keep from falling. I started talking somewhat incoherently.

"I need help. I'm sick. My name's Packy. Please, I don't need to come inside, but could you somehow get me help?"

"What's wrong?" She asked.

"I have a pneumonia. I've walked all the way from Montana. I came across the border."

I immediately knew that was the wrong thing to say. She would now be suspicious, more so than she probably already was. I stumbled on my words, trying to convince her, but instead I knew I was making things worse.

"I have a book, a Bigfoot book, and I need help getting rid of it, so they came with me, they helped me, Hap and the White One brought me here, they said you could help me..."

She was now outside on the porch, holding my arm, keeping me from collapsing, helping me into the house. Wagger was right next to me, following along.

"Geez, what a cute dog, but what a mess," she said, ignoring everything I'd just said. "Look, let's get you into a room, then we can figure out what to do. My name's Lisa."

Lisa led me through the living room, where a well-dressed couple was sitting drinking coffee. I nodded my head to them in greeting, nearly tripping over their feet.

"Steady, now," Lisa cautioned. "Good morning, Mr. and Mrs. Gullette. This man just hiked across the Rockies. We're getting him into a cozy room where he can get cleaned up and rested."

"That's Wagger," I said to the couple, trying to be congenial. "He came across the border, too. In fact, we crossed illegally. On foot. With Tracker chasing us. He's a Bigfoot."

My lungs were hurting again and I started coughing uncontrollably.

"Illegally? Bigfoot?" asked the well-dressed woman with concern.

"He was sick and lost," Lisa said, smiling a strained smile. She then led me up the stairs and into a room that looked out over a beautiful garden surrounding a small pond.

"Look," she said. "You're really sick. You stay put, get into bed, and I'll bring you some breakfast. We'll work out the details later on the price."

I slumped onto the bed. It felt like a big fluffy down pillow. I couldn't even remember the last time I'd been in a bed. It felt weird, like I should get up before I got it all dirty. I stood back up.

Lisa said, "Look, Packy, do you have any clean clothes? I mean, that t-shirt looks like you got it in Tibet and haven't washed it since."

I looked down at my shirt. All that could now be read of the "Free Tibet" was "Tibet."

Lisa continued, "I'll bring you something—we always have a few things around that people left. If you want to take a shower, there's a robe on the door in the bathroom. Just relax and don't worry about a thing. I'll be back with breakfast for you and the little dog, too. Do you mind if I give him a bath?"

I nodded my head OK.

Lisa continued, but in a low voice, "Did the White Ones really bring you here?"

I nodded yes, then asked, "Where am I?"

"You're in a little town called Fernie," Lisa replied, then was silent.

"Can you thoughtcast?" she cast to me.

I answered, "A thought just popped into my head from nowhere."

She smiled, leaving me to ponder this turn in my fortunes.

CHAPTER 45

I had managed to take a long hot shower, one that left me feeling much better, even though I had to stand and cough for ten minutes to clear my lungs from all the steam.

I was afraid to look in the mirror, and when I did, I didn't recognize myself. I looked like a wraith. I was thin and had a scraggly beard and long hair. OK, I'd already had the scraggly beard and hair, but it all looked longer—and worse.

Lisa had left me some clean clothes—a pair of sweat pants that were a bit baggy and a t-shirt with the words, "Bigfoot is Blurry."

I had collapsed onto the bed and was resting when a knock came at the door. It was Lisa, with a tray filled with all kinds of food that I'd forgotten existed—quiche and fruit and miniature pancake thingies that she called crepes— well, maybe food I actually had never known existed. I kind of wished Hap were there to share it with me, but not really, given his propensity to eat everything in sight.

Lisa also had Wagger, who instantly began rolling on the carpet from his bath, but who then stopped long enough to eat some of the quiche.

"Feeling better?" she asked.

"Yes, thanks. I really appreciate your help, but you need to know I only have about $100 in my jeans, wherever they are."

"In the wash."

"Thanks. You can keep any money you find."

She laughed, then became serious. "You have a pneumonia? We need to get you to a doctor. Problem is, if you're here illegally, you won't have an ID card, and they won't treat you."

"Why not? I need antibiotics."

"It's our medical system here. Every citizen gets free care, but you have to be a Canadian."

"What about non-Canadians that get sick while they're here? Do they just die?"

"No, no, but they need to have passports and health insurance from their own country. Do you have a passport? If not, I imagine they would treat you, but then deport you. But I have a friend who's a doctor. Let me call him. No promises, though."

"No promises," I replied, leaning back onto the bed. I felt better, but was still lightheaded. Lisa handed me a cup of hot tea and left.

I locked the door, then pulled the Book of Runes from where I'd hidden it under my pillow. I slowly opened it.

It was a bit lighter, as I'd used it more than once for firestarter—in fact, most of the book was missing by then. I guess I felt like if I had to carry it and go through all the trouble it had caused, I was free to utilize its resources, so to say.

I turned to the back and carefully ripped out the maps, one by one, then wrapped what was left of the book in my jacket and put it back under my pillow.

Wagger was now sleeping on the other pillow, and I reached out and ran my hand over his shiny yellow coat.

"Wow, I mean bow wow, Wagger, you're something else, eh? Nice and pretty now. Nobody would ever know you're an alien, an illegal alien."

Wagger wagged his tail and licked my hand. I got up and walked over to the window, where I held the three maps up to the light. I had to realign them several times, and it took me a minute to process what I was seeing.

The translucent paper was almost glowing, and on it I could now make out writings in ink, which I hadn't noticed before. I couldn't read them, as they were in runes, but I could make out what looked like a scene one would see from an airplane—mountains and valleys and rivers and a dark line that threaded through it all, maybe showing a route. It looked kind of like a primitive 3D map.

But a route to where? Some of the mountains had runes on them as if to identify them, and I was able to make out a line that reminded me of the China Wall, which helped me get my bearings.

A river ran through a long valley that separated the two huge mountain ranges. I then realized that the river could very well be the mighty Kootenay, which was very close to where I was.

As I studied it more, I found landmarks that helped orient me until I finally figured out that I was indeed looking at a map of the exact region where I now stood.

How could we be so lucky, Hap and I, to come to the place we needed to be? I then recalled Hap's recollections of his childhood, which I had questioned, and I knew that his memory had been right.

But where was this so-called Place Where the Sun Lingers, this Bigfoot heritage site? It might be identified on the map, but until I learned to read runes, I would never know.

I studied the map some more, then discovered that if I held the three pieces a bit further apart, the 3D effect increased. It was a very clever thing, this map, something I could picture only a society of explorers like the Vikings inventing, people who must have loved and revered maps.

And now the mountains seemed to show more height. I tracked the line, the possible route, as it went along the peaks of the mountains in the Columbia Range, touching peaks in the Caribou and the Monashee, then the Selkirks and Purcells. Soon, the line stopped, and was marked by a rune that I took to mean X marks the spot.

But where exactly was that spot? I knew it had to be the Place Where the Sun Lingers, but how could I possibly place it among so many large mountains?

I needed another set of eyes, someone who knew those mountains, maybe a climber.

Just then, a knock came at the door from someone who would soon answer my questions.

CHAPTER 46

"Packy, this is my good friend, Dr. Jake."

Lisa led a tall man into the room who looked to be in his mid-forties. He was dressed like someone ready to go hiking, in khaki shorts, hiking shoes, and a loud red and yellow Hawaiian shirt.

"Hi, Packy, what's going on? I hear you may have a pneumonia."

He began taking stuff from a little black bag and was soon taking my temperature, listening to my lungs, and taking my blood pressure.

I didn't say a word, as I didn't want to disrupt his checkup. Finally, he turned to Lisa and said, "I think pneumonia is right. His lungs sound pretty bad, even though he doesn't seem to have a really high fever."

"Doc, the fever broke yesterday," I said. "But now I'm really tired and weak and I cough a lot."

"I'm going to leave you some antibiotics." Doc Jake pulled out a bottle of pills. "Azithromycin, the big guns. I don't know if it's a viral or bacterial pneumonia without doing tests, but this will keep any side problems from developing. Take one a day for seven days. You'll start feeling better in a day or two. I'll also leave a bottle of cough syrup with codeine in it. It's a controlled substance, so don't give it to anyone else."

I was already feeling better, maybe just from the attention. The doc was ready to go, and Lisa was thanking him for stopping by, when I piped up.

"Doc, are you an outdoorsman, a hiker maybe or climber?"

He looked surprised. "Yes, how did you know?"

"It's the Hawaiian shirt thing," I answered, though I had only guessed. "I'm wondering if you could show me a couple of things on a map real quick. Lisa, do you have a map of this area, one that shows the mountains?"

Lisa was soon back with an atlas. She opened it, and I pointed to the area where the rune had marked the spot on the runes map.

"What's here?" I asked.

Jake took a close look, then said, "That's the Bugaboos."

I replied, "The Bugaboos? Now there's a name. Isn't a bugaboo a bogeyman? But is there something there that's really big, I mean a big landmark or something?"

Jake laughed. "Yeah, it's all big. It was once called the Nunataks, which is an Inuit word for an exposed ridge or peak in the middle of an ice field. That describes the Bugaboos perfectly. Some call them the Bugaboo Spires, but the big one is called that, so I just call them the Bugaboos, or the Bugs."

"Why are they called the Bugaboos?"

"The old-time gold miners called them that. Maybe they saw lots of bugaboos up there."

Lisa and I both looked at each other knowingly. I said, "Maybe. You ever go up in there much?"

Jake replied, "I used to. I even climbed the Houndstooth and Bugaboo Spire, but I had something happen that scared me off. Funny, but I thought I saw a Bigfoot, but it was white. Maybe it was an Abominable Snowman. I never talk about this, so please don't repeat it. My patients would think I was nutty. But I quit going up there after that. Funny, but I never thought much about the name..."

"Me neither," said Lisa. "Bugaboo—Bigfoot. I know others who have seen them up there."

"Are they granite? The Bugaboos, I mean." I thought of Hap recollecting a big granite spire.

"Yes. See, technically, they're part of the Columbia Mountains, the Purcell Range. The Rocky Mountain Trench splits them from the Canadian Rockies proper. Invermere sits in the Trench. The original ancient Purcells were really old sedimentary rock, but more recent masses of molten rock pierced through them and cooled into hard granite."

"Batholiths," I interrupted. "Same as in Yosemite. Huge walls and spires. Crystalline granodiorite batholiths. Then the outer layers eroded away, leaving the spires."

Jake looked surprised. "You sound like a geologist."

"I used to be one, long ago. Would like to be one again someday."

Jake added, "I have a friend who said he heard chanting one night—scared the crap out of him. He left and won't go back."

"Well, Doc, you're not the only one in the room who's seen Bigfoot, so not to worry," I said. "Thanks for your help."

"Yeah, Thanks for coming, Jake," Lisa added. "You know you and Janna can come stay here anytime you want for free."

"Thanks, Lisa, but we're fine. And maybe sometime you can tell me your Bigfoot story," he nodded to me.

"Sure, when it's over," I answered.

He smiled, opened the door, and left.

"Now you can tell me more about why you're here, Packy," Lisa said, sitting in a chair by the window. "Assuming you want to, that is."

I answered, "I don't know why I'm here. They just brought me here, that's all."

"No, I don't mean here literally, I mean in British Columbia. How did you land here in Fernie?"

"I had a Bigfoot escort," I answered.

Lisa sighed. "OK, if you don't want to tell me, that's fine. It's none of my business, really—I was just curious. You know, I had a white Bigfoot come here once injured and I helped it. It taught me to thoughtcast."

"What was wrong with it?"

"I don't know."

"How did you help it?"

"It was out by the pond, just hanging out there because of the water, I guess. I saw it in the bushes and went to see what it was. It couldn't move. I was terrified, but I knew it needed help. I started bringing it water, then food. That took a lot of courage for me, I can tell you. It started putting thoughts into my mind, then it told me how to do the same until we started communicating. I was able to tend to it until it got better. It looked like it had been hit by a car or something."

"That's a crazy story, and I'm not sure I believe it," I replied.

Lisa looked surprised, then started laughing. She came over and squeezed my shoulder.

"Start taking those antibiotics. It was good of Jake to come here, he could lose his job if anyone found out. I'll be back with some dinner, then we can talk some more. I'm taking Wagger downstairs with me so we can go for a little walk."

"I'll be here when you get back," I replied. I then thoughtcast to her, "And keep an eye out for Tracker. He's a really mean Bigfoot, and he's looking for me."

Lisa cast back, "I'll be careful, Packy. Get some rest."

CHAPTER 47

I spent a number of wonderful days resting and recovering at the Fernwood Bed and Breakfast, and Lisa and I spent a lot of time talking, especially about Bigfoot.

I told her my story and all about the Book of Runes. When I told her about Tracker, she worried, but I assured her that Tracker was pretty unlikely to come around any place where there were humans.

I was finally getting to where I felt pretty close to normal, though I was still weak at times. I hadn't taken any of the antibiotics, as I knew I would be better now that the fever had broken and I had a warm place to stay, and I've never liked taking medicine unless it was really necessary.

I had stuck the pills and the cough syrup in my jacket pocket and basically forgotten about them.

Wagger loved Lisa and took to following her around. At first I felt left out, but then I realized he was getting what he needed and what I hadn't been able to give—security and stability, all wrapped up into one person. I toyed with the idea of leaving him there, as I knew my stay was temporary.

Hap would return any day, wanting to know the secret of the maps, and I had to help him see this through to the very end, even though I still wasn't so sure what we were seeing through or what the end would be.

But by about the tenth day and no Hap, I was beginning to worry. To be honest, I hoped he would never return, as I was happy to stay where I was, but I knew I would worry about him until he did.

By day eleven, I was wondering what to do. I asked Lisa.

"Should I call the animal shelter and see if he's been picked up?" I joked.

"They'll want to know if he's been microchipped," she laughed back. "And want a photo. Don't worry, he'll show up."

I thought about this later. If I had taken a photo of him, I'd be a rich man now. But given how the camera at Blacktail had failed, I doubt if any camera could've taken that photo, and even if it had, the skeptics would probably debunk it.

Finally, on the evening of the fourteenth day, I heard Hap casting to me. I answered.

"Hap! You OK?"

"Hap fine. And Packy better?"

"Packy much better. Hap, I figured out the map. Where are you?"

I was standing by my window, looking for him.

"Hap in the bushes. Can see Packy. I have a White One with me. We all go now, Packy."

"Hap, I can't go yet. I'm still too weak to walk that far. Look, it's a long ways, but I can get a ride in a car and meet you there."

"Where?"

"Hap, it's what we call the Bugaboos. Go there and wait for me."

"Hap don't know Bugaboos."

"The Nunataks."

"Nunataks? Hap know Nunataks. Where Hap was born. The Place Where the Sun Lingers. Where is it?"

Now Hap stood directly under my window, and I tossed the maps down to him. I told him how to orient them and hold them to the sun, which he did. He was soon all excited like a little kid.

"Hap see Nunataks now, Packy. Long ways off and many mountains. Bigfoot walk, take maybe ten suns. We meet you there, Packy, ten days."

"I'll be there, Hap, with the book."

"Hap will thoughtcast for Bigfoot to come to Nunataks for big meeting at the Place Where the Sun Lingers. Will be many there. Soon, Packy, as you humans say, soon we will be free."

"Hap, you're already free, you know that," I cast. "But yes, it will be a big change. We'll destroy the book and it'll be a big Bigfoot Reformation. We'll ride the train to freedom. Don't need no tickets, you just get on board."

"What?"

"Never mind, Hap."

I was glad Lisa didn't have any guests yet for the day, as I knew Hap would be seen. It was time for him to go.

"Packy?"

"Yeah?"

"Tracker's nearby. Be careful. He's wounded. Hamumu and Gwa'wina have been watching him. Accident with death flinger, shot himself in the foot."

"Was it the same foot he injured in the car crash?"

"Hap don't know."

"Doesn't he know guns are illegal in Canada?"

"Hap don't know. Hap go now."
"Be safe."

CHAPTER 48

I didn't sleep well that night, and I wasn't sure if it was from coughing or because I was thinking of Tracker or from the woodknocking I thought I heard.

Wagger had taken to sleeping with Lisa, and I missed having him around to tell me if something was wrong. I could've taken him back, but I wanted Lisa to be safe.

Sure enough, I was standing looking out my window early the next morning when someone cast to me, "Packy, Tracker's nearby."

It was Hamumu.

I saw a black form over in the trees by the pond. Even though it was barely dawn and I really couldn't see much, I knew it was Tracker.

I quickly got dressed, grabbed my jacket, which had the book stuffed in it, and went downstairs where Lisa was making coffee.

Lisa asked, "What's up?"

"Well," I answered, "I think it's time I asked you out on a date. Let's go into town, or somewhere, anywhere you want to go. I'll buy you breakfast. But let's do it right now."

"A date? But I don't want to go anywhere, and why would we go on a date?" She looked at me funny, then asked, "What's going on? Is something wrong? Should I call the RCMP?"

"What's that?" I asked.

"The Mounties."

"No, no, Lisa, don't do that. I can explain. Look, I'm stupid, and I always say the wrong things, just expect that from now on and it will make things easier for you. But I just got a message from my Bigfoot friend, Hamumu. Tracker's nearby."

"What?"

"We need to leave."

"I thought you weren't afraid of Tracker."

"Sometimes I say things that aren't true hoping that if I say them enough they'll be true," I replied. "Besides, he has my gun."

Lisa looked alarmed and grabbed her jacket and pickup keys.

"Let's go," she said.

I was right behind her, then stopped and thought for a moment, grabbing her arm.

"Lisa, you're right. I can't run anymore. I have to stand up to him."

"You can't stand up to a Bigfoot."

"I'll stand up next to him, then," I replied, trying to smile. "Keep Wagger in here. I'll cast you if anything goes wrong."

"What should I do then?"

"I dunno, run like hell, I guess. Or call the Mounties."

I opened the back door and went into the yard, then to the pond. I sat down on a big rock, pretending I didn't know Tracker was there, and started whistling "Row, row, row your boat..."

Nothing. I expected Tracker to charge me or something, but there was nothing. I could see Lisa looking out from behind the curtain in my bedroom upstairs, Wagger in her arms.

"Life is but a dream..."

Maybe he was going to shoot me and was targeting me in. Finally, I heard a moaning sound. I knew it was Tracker. I got up and went over to the trees, where he was on his back, moaning, obviously in pain.

"What's up, Tracker?" I cast.

"Tracker want book," he moaned, unable to get up.

"They'll kill you, don't you believe me? Where's the death flinger?"

"In lake."

"You shot your foot? Let me see it, Tracker. I can help."

I went over next to him and bent over, looking at his foot. He easily could've killed me with one blow, but I somehow knew he wouldn't. He needed help. His foot was a bloody mess.

I remembered the medicine in my jacket pocket. I took out the antibiotics, opened the lid, and handed it to him.

"Eat this. It will help your foot heal."

I knew it was a seven day supply for me, but I weighed about one-fifth what Tracker did, if even that, so I figured it would be about one or two day's worth for him. He swallowed all the pills at once.

"Here, chase it down with this."

I handed him the bottle of cough syrup. I knew the codeine would help take the edge off the pain—or at least I hoped so, as I had no idea if a Bigfoot had a similar body chemistry to humans. Based on what I'd been thinking earlier about their molecular structure, they probably didn't, but it was worth a try. At the very least, it would kill him and end all the drama.

"It's a controlled substance, so don't give it to anyone else," I cast as Tracker drank the whole bottle down at once.

"What?" Tracker cast.

"Never mind. So, you still want that damn book, eh? Where are the people who are telling you they'll take good care of you, Tracker? Why aren't they helping you now that you're injured?"

Tracker said nothing.

"Look, I have a friend who will clean your foot if you'll let her and promise not to harm her."

"Tracker be good."

I cast to Lisa, and she was soon there, carefully cleaning Tracker's foot while I handed her stuff and watched, being my typical helpful but incompetent self.

I had been a medic, for crying out loud, but this simple task seemed beyond me. I felt like it was triggering some old memory, my PTSD.

But suddenly, I felt detached, carefree. It was like I was in a hot-air balloon, lifting off, and Tracker and Lisa were getting smaller and smaller below me, until they were just dots, and then Fernie and the Canadian Rockies were just dots in a vast landscape as if I were in outer space, orbiting the earth.

I then realized that nothing really mattered to me, we were all together in this, floating through the emptiness of space on a very small planet, whirling forever into a void none of us could ever comprehend.

I unwrapped the Book of Runes from my jacket and handed it to Tracker. He looked shocked, as did Lisa.

"Here, it's yours. See how easy that was? No need to fight—there's nothing in it worth fighting over."

Tracker gingerly took the book, then lay it down as if it would burn his fingers if he held it for very long.

Lisa was now done with his foot.

I cast, "Tracker, your foot will heal now, but be careful. The book is now your burden. You must take it to the Nunataks in nine days. You'll be a hero to your own kind. It's a reformation, a new life, and the book must be destroyed. Promise you'll be there."

Tracker just sat there, silent. I could tell the codeine was affecting him.

Now Lisa cast, "Tracker, my people will kill you after they get the book."

This seemed to surprise Tracker, as if he didn't know she could thoughtcast.

Tracker frowned, then cast, "Tracker do what Tracker wants. Tracker could kill you, but won't. But maybe Tracker will kill the humans who want the book. Maybe Tracker will keep the book for himself."

"What's the point?" I asked.

"Tracker needs no point because he Otaktay, Kills Many."

"Maybe you should change your name," Lisa said in disgust, walking back to the house, then turned to ask, "How about changing it to BMOC?"

"Tracker don't know BMOC," he answered, puzzled.

"Big Man on Campus, Tracker," I cast. "It seems to suit you, for some reason. A campus is like a town. You're a Big Man, or Big Bigfoot would be more like it. Big Bigfoot on Campus, BBOC."

Tracker showed his teeth as I turned to go. I thought he might be smiling, but I wasn't sure, though I figured the irony was lost on him.

And as I walked away, he screamed a scream that would raise the dead. It was scary—but not scary enough, I decided, and kept on walking without looking back.

I wondered if I'd done the right thing in giving him the book—and I wondered if he would notice all the pages were now gone, used as firestarter, leaving nothing but the leather binding.

CHAPTER 49

Lisa and I had spent the morning running the B&B, she tending to guests while I helped do the laundry and clean and other macho man stuff.

We had talked some about Tracker, and I could see he was gone, hopefully on his way to the Place Where the Sun Lingers, where I hoped he, too, would linger and not come back.

I wasn't sure what I would do if Tracker didn't show up for the big day there, but Lisa had a plan. She was going to take me up there, as close as her pickup would get, then we'd hike in the rest of the way. I was feeling better, but wasn't so sure I could do the hike, but we would see.

She had spent the afternoon making a substitute for the Book of Runes just in case we needed it, using a big thick book she'd picked up at the local library sale, something called "Fernie Ice Hockey Greats."

When she was done it looked pretty authentic, like the real Book of Runes, as long as you didn't open it, but I was hoping Tracker would show up for the big event and we wouldn't have to use it. I had no idea what Hap would say about all this.

Finally, after dinner and all the guests had been settled in, Lisa pulled me aside and said, "I know just the place for you—someplace where you can get some rest and nobody will bother you."

I wasn't sure if this meant a nice cozy corner in some library or someplace at the bottom of a lake wearing cement shoes, but I obediently followed to her pickup, Wagger in my arms. I would just have to trust her. She brought the replica Book of Runes so I could take a better look at it on the way.

It would be the first time I'd been away from the house, and the town of Fernie was a pleasant surprise to me. I loved the way it was surrounded by towering picturesque mountains, which were now pink with alpenglow from the setting sun.

I was falling in love with the Canadian Rockies, which were much different from those in Colorado, though technically not as tall. But they had a bigger rise from base to top and seemed much more rugged and untouched, my kind of place.

I had no idea where we were going, but I was enjoying the scenery. We seemed to be heading downhill, away from what I later found out was Crowsnest Pass, which crossed on over into the Calgary region.

Before long, Lisa turned off onto a small forest road and the pickup began climbing and climbing, following a small stream. It was nearly dark, and I was a bit worried about where she was taking us. I really didn't relish the thought of being out in the deep forest all alone—been there, done that.

But we soon stopped at a kind of pullout, and I could see what looked like a hot springs, with several small pools along the edge of the creek below us.

I was soon in the water, which Lisa said was called Penny Hot Springs because people used to throw pennies in it. I sat and soaked while she sat on the edge, playing stick with Wagger.

The water felt so soothing, so good, and I could feel my tensions and worries fading away. It reminded me of what seemed like a long time ago when Hap and I had soaked in the Glenwood Hot Springs, hiding from Tracker. Funny, how my fears of Tracker had faded, just like my worries faded in that warm calming water.

"This was a good idea," I cast. For some reason, I didn't want to talk and break the silence. Maybe it was some kind of survival instinct.

Lisa apparently understood, as she cast back, "This used to be a historic place for the Bigfoot to come soak. There are hot springs all over this area, but the Bigfoot don't come to them so much, as we've pretty much taken the springs over."

"How do you know all that?"

"The White One, Kup, Little Owl, told me. The one I helped."

"What language is Kup?"

"Ktunaxa, spoken by the Kootenay People here in B.C., or Kootenai in Montana."

"So, the White Ones are from here?"

"Yes, they're locals. They wear white baseball hats that say 'BC Native.' You have to look close, cause the hats blend in."

I smiled. "Why do you suppose they're white?"

"There's a whole band of them, Kup told me, all from around the Bugaboos. I think they evolved the white coat because it's so snowy and icy around there. She said they

call themselves the First Voices because they were the first
Bigfoot to cross over."

"Cross over what?"

"I guess the Bering Straits. Maybe they're related to the
Abominable Snowman."

"I wonder how Hap fits in with all that. He's not white,
yet his Greats are highly revered, and he said he was born
here."

"There are other bands, but they range, so they adapted
to the forest colors."

"You mean there are green Bigfoot?" I asked.

Lisa laughed out loud, and suddenly, the forest was
still. An ominous feeling immediately came over us both.
Lisa turned pale—or maybe it was from the rising moon—
and I knew we were being watched. The hairs on my neck
would've stood up, but they were too wet.

Lisa grabbed Wagger as I jumped from the hot springs,
pulling on a dry t-shirt she'd brought that had the words,
"Question Authority" on it.

Lisa cast, "Who's there?"

There was no response, but I could see shadows moving. I was worried it might be a grizzly bear, but soon a
whole group of Bigfoot stepped from the trees.

I counted six. I'd never seen so many together before,
and they were just like humans in that they were different
sizes and had different features. Two looked to be young
children. They were all dark, so I assumed they were some
of the ones Hap had put out the call to and weren't locals.

Now the largest in the group stood forward and cast,
"How is it you can thoughtcast? Are you enemy or friend?"

Lisa answered, "Friend, even though human. The old ways are over, and humans and Bigfoot can now be friends."

"Let's all be friends," I cast hopefully. We were seriously outnumbered and outgunned.

No one spoke for awhile. I was starting to get nervous, so I cast, "I'm Packy, Bearer of the Book of Runes. This is Lisa, Holder of Wagger, and Wagger, He Who Wags When Lisa Holds."

I held out my arm, just as I'd seen Hap do. "Let us grasp arms or whatever you guys call it and be friends, you know, that 'I hold your arm with good feelings in my heart' thingy you guys do."

For some reason, the tension dissipated, and I could now see Lisa smiling, but I had a strong suspicion she was smiling at me and not with me—but it didn't matter, as long as everyone was smiling.

Now the big one stepped forward, holding out his arm, and said, "I am Naxni, Caribou. I hold your arm with good feelings in my heart."

He grasped arms with Lisa and then me, then the next one came up.

"I am Wakuks, Gray Jay. I hold your arm with good feelings in my heart."

"I am Nasayit, Wood Lily. I hold your arm with good feelings in my heart."

"I am Nupqu, Bear. I hold your arm with good feelings in my heart."

Now the two little ones stepped forward.

"I am Mata, Mint. I hold your arm with good feelings in my heart."

"I am Waxwik, Dragon Fly. I hold your arm with good feelings in my heart."

"Well," I cast, "Since there are so many good feelings in the air, why don't you join us in the hot springs and tell us where you're going?"

Nupqu cast, "We are going to the Nunataks, where we've been told the Book of Runes will be destroyed. Since you're the bearer, is this true?"

I hesitated. For some reason, I felt a sense of hostility in his casting.

"Yes, it's true. Are you a Teacher, by any chance?"

"Yes," was the answer. "I'm Nupqu, Head Teacher of the Bigfoot Tribe. And I intend to see the book restored, not destroyed."

CHAPTER 50

"Are you one of the hoodlums who sent Tracker after me to get the book at any cost, including my life?" I cast to Nupqu, angry.

He was now sitting across the hot springs from me, his head back, relaxed, as the others also sat in the steamy pool, their long shaggy arm-hair floating in the hot water.

Lisa sat by the side of the pool, next to me, holding Wagger, and I could see a strained look on her face.

I'd been sitting there in the steam, at first kind of enjoying myself, until the anger started surfacing, getting hotter and hotter like lava, then finally erupting.

Nupqu quickly sat up, looking threatened. He then relaxed a bit and answered, "Yes. Nupqu don't know hoodlum, but yes, Nupqu wants the book back."

"So, you've walked all the way from Colorado, from the Rune Cave?"

I could tell Nupqu didn't like being interrogated, probably wasn't used to it, being the head honcho and all, but I didn't care.

To be sitting there looking straight at the one who'd put a price on my head, well, it just made me livid to no end. In fact, I was beginning to feel a rage, as if I were back in the war. I was holding him responsible for all the pain I'd felt since taking the book from the cave.

Nupqu must've sensed this, as he cast, "Nupqu will honor the arm grasping, will Packy? Nupqu comes from Flathead, not Colorado."

"Maybe I'll honor it," I cast back, "If you want to be honest with me. Your minions are in Colorado, then?"

"Packy have death flinger?"

"Maybe, maybe not. It doesn't matter. You put a contract on my head, and I'm angry."

"Nupqu don't know contract."

"Dammit, you Bigfoot don't know squat, do you?"

"Nupqu knows Squatch."

He nodded his head towards his fellow Bigfoot, who were all very quiet. I wasn't sure if they could read our thoughtcasts, but they seemed to at least sense what was going on.

Now Lisa spoke to me out loud so the Bigfoot wouldn't understand, "Packy, let's go. We're seriously outnumbered."

"Will everyone here honor the arm grasping?" I cast, pretending I hadn't heard her.

They all nodded their heads sideways, which I knew meant yes.

"We're OK, Lisa, for now, anyway," I said out loud.

I continued casting. "Is this your family, Nupqu?"

"Yes."

"They're beautiful."

"Thank you," he replied.

"Why do you want them to live in superstition and fear?"

"Do they look fearful?" he cast back.

I could tell he knew exactly what I was talking about—
the superstitions in the book.

I got out of the hot springs, dried off, then went to the
truck. Nupqu watched me like a hawk, also getting out. I
knew he'd heard that I had a death flinger, and he obviously didn't know Tracker had shot himself and thrown the
gun into a lake.

"Packy have death flinger?" he cast again. His family
now started nervously getting out of the pool.

"See, Nupqu, that's fear. You all have fear, right now,
yes, you all look scared to death. You think I'm going to
fling death at you. That's fear. But no, I'm not going to shoot
you, I'm going to show you something."

I reached into the truck and pulled out the new Book
of Runes that Lisa had just made. I held it up in the moonlight, and, just as I figured, everyone stepped back.

I felt like some dark lord in a movie who had just picked
up a deathly laser gun or some vampire hunter holding up
a cross. They all looked terrified, even Nupqu.

I walked forward, still holding up the book, and they
all walked backwards, away from me. I felt like I had some
mystical power all of a sudden, and it hit me then and there
what drove Nupqu and his kind—power. Wanting power
over others. It was despicable, and I had no tolerance for it.

"You take the common and turn it into the sacred so
you can control others with it, don't you, Nupqu? That's the
role you've chosen as a Teacher. But a real teacher does just
the opposite, enlightens. You prefer to keep minds in the
darkness so you can control them. You're a monster."

I will admit that I saw the irony in calling a Bigfoot a
monster, but I didn't stop. I was talking to the Bigfoot who

had sent Tracker to kill me, and I was justifiably angry, even though Tracker was really after the book for his own purposes, although Nupqu didn't know that.

Nupqu cast, "You're a hypocrite, Packy. You humans yourself have a saying, 'Ask too many questions and we'll kill the cat.' That's not seeking enlightenment."

I had to stop and think for awhile, but then I cast back, "You mean, 'Curiosity killed the cat.' But it was originally 'Care, or worry, killed the cat.' And don't forget, cats have nine lives, so they can explore whatever they want."

Nupqu looked confused. I continued, "You're the opposite of what you claim to be, Nupqu, and this book has caused your kind much pain and despair, and yet you continue to teach its ways so you can hold power in your hands, pretending you're something you're not—a real teacher."

I had been casting to everyone, and I could tell they understood, for they all looked horrified, except for the kids, who just looked scared. That kind of got to me, as I'm not into scaring kids, so I tried to calm down.

Now, quietly, I cast solely to Nupqu, "I know your kind. You're really a coward underneath it all, aren't you? I can prove it."

I stepped towards him, holding out the fake Book of Runes.

"Here, Nupqu, take the book. You wanted it, take it. No need for Otaktay to kill me."

Nupqu stepped backwards, frightened. It was then that I decided he must really believe the hype about the book. He was born into it and must believe it, even while using it for his own unscrupulous purposes.

"It's not sacred, Nupqu, it's just a book. Take it."
I pressed it into his big hands.

Nupqu fell to his knees and started hyperventilating as if he'd been hit by electricity.

"See, you're not dead. It's all a lie."

Nupqu slowly stood, still holding the book, looking shocked. He gingerly held the book up to examine it, turning it over and looking at the cover.

I finally reached to take it back, and he calmly let it go. I then turned to the two kids, who looked to be young, maybe about five or six.

"Always question authority," I cast, pointing to my shirt. "Think for yourself."

I knew they had no idea what was going on. I turned to the others and cast, "See you at the Bugaboos. Maybe we'll have a pancake dinner after it's all over. If any of you play drums, bring them and we'll have a big drum circle."

Then I casually tossed the book into the hot springs.

With that, Lisa, Wagger, and I got into the pickup, and the three of us drove on down the road.

"A place where I won't be bothered, eh?" I teased.

"Dammit, it took me all afternoon to make that book," Lisa replied, half-laughing with relief.

I put my arm around her shoulders as she drove on home in the moonlight.

CHAPTER 51

The next few days were uneventful, just more helping Lisa run her B&B and that kind of thing.

I wondered how Hap was doing, knowing he was walking to the Bugaboos, which was a long walk—I guesstimated around 200 miles by road, but maybe a bit closer as the crow flies. Given the speed I'd seen him move, I knew he could easily make it.

I wondered if Tracker could even do the hike, but then remembered he maybe still had humans helping him—but maybe not, given the condition of his foot, as they sure hadn't helped him any there.

He could even be dead by now, from the looks of his wound. But maybe the antibiotics and cleaning had helped.

Lisa and I finally started gathering camping gear a couple of days before we were set to leave. I wasn't looking forward to going to the Bugaboos, and I had no idea what role I would play in the whole thing now that the Book of Runes was gone.

It all seemed really futile and even a bit ridiculous at this point, and I wondered how Hap would take it that I'd given the book to Tracker, what was left of it, anyway.

I guess he couldn't trust me after all, and it made me feel bad. And just because it meant nothing to me, it was a big deal to him and his kind.

Oh well, I figured, you can't look back too far or your whole life is steeped with regret—at least mine was, anyway.

But I thought about it a bunch. I no longer had the book, but I decided to have something that would far surpass anything Hap could bring to the show, book or no. I wasn't sure how I was going to do it, but I had the inklings of a plan—but I would have to act quickly.

I told Lisa what I was thinking and she got on the internet, placing an overnight rush order. We would have a big surprise for the Bigfoot gathering.

As time went on, Lisa and I soon stopped discussing Bigfoot, the common interest that had brought us together and been a mutual bond, and began talking about other things.

It seemed we both loved animals and the outdoors, and she, too had been through a relationship that hadn't worked out. We had a lot in common and were beginning to enjoy each other's company.

The morning before what I was now calling the Bigfoot Reformation, we loaded everything in Lisa's pickup, then headed out. It was early, and a feeling of trepidation filled us both. We had decided to leave Wagger home with a friend of Lisa's, and he was all too happy to curl up by the fireplace.

We headed west down the valley on the Crowsnest Highway to the intersection with Highway 93, then on to Cranbrook, to the Columbia Highway. We were now going pretty much due north.

We drove along the bank of beautiful Lake Columbia, the headwaters of the Kootenay River, the beginnings of the mighty Columbia River that later courses through Washington. This was all new country to me, and I was enjoying seeing it.

The Rocky Mountain Rift, which we were driving through, was bounded by high mountains that were rugged and wild, snowcapped peaks that summer hadn't yet touched. I knew a number of them had permanent glaciers, and some of the snow was new.

It was a long trip, and each time we would stop for a break, I wondered where Hap was.

We eventually reached Windermere Lake and the town of Invermere, which sat on the lake shore. There, we stopped and drove down by the lake, where we got out and stretched our legs, eating lunch and feeding the gulls.

We were soon back on the road, and before long we arrived in Radium Hot Springs, where we stopped for gas. The actual hot springs were up the road on the Kootenay Highway, a beautiful drive that went on over to the Lake Louise region. I later became more familiar with all this country, but that's getting ahead of the story.

It was a short drive further north to the small settlement of Brisco, where we got on the Brisco Road, crossing the Kootenay River, which was pale blue from glacial till. We saw a sign that read "Bugaboo Provincial Park."

The road to the Bugaboos was a well-used logging road, and I was glad that logging season hadn't yet started, as there were places where it didn't seem wide enough for both a vehicle and a logging truck.

It seemed like it took forever to gradually climb up the valley we were now following, and I worried that we would eventually reach snowbanks and be stopped.

After about an hour or so, we came to a turnoff with a sign that read, "CMH Bugaboo Lodge." This was a luxury lodge used by hikers and climbers, though still closed for the season. We continued on up the main road, which at that point became rough and slow going, though it fortunately wasn't snowed in.

We finally reached the end of the road, where we parked in a small parking lot.

Lisa took a roll of chicken wire from the back of the truck and, after we had unloaded our gear, wrapped it around the base of the pickup.

"What's that for?" I asked.

"Doc Jake told me to use it up here. Porcupines and other critters will chew on the brakelines and tires."

I helped her wrap the truck, then we hoisted our packs and started up the trail, where another sign pointed us towards the Conrad Kain Hut, an overnight hut for hikers and climbers that was built right at the base of the Bugaboo Glacier, one of the big icefields surrounding the spires.

Far above us, I could see the hut—a little teal-colored speck beneath a huge granite needle called the Snowpatch Spire. It looked a lot further than three miles away, and I felt deflated.

We were now a mile high in altitude, according to Lisa, and would climb another 2400 feet to get to the hut. I wondered if I was strong enough to make the hike, as that's where we planned to overnight, even though it too was still closed for the season.

We would have to break into the building, but we decided that would be better than trying to camp outdoors in the cold, especially with a tribe of Bigfoot nearby, most who we guessed would not be overly friendly.

Earlier, back at the B&B, Lisa had showed me what her internet research had revealed about the hike to the hut.

"The trail climbs three miles through granite bluffs and follows the northern lateral moraine of Bugaboo Glacier and is very steep and strenuous, with exposure on steep drop-offs and cliffs. The ladder and hand cables may be difficult for those with a fear of heights. Extreme caution is advised, and strong, reliable footwear is essential."

I closed the pickup door and sighed, shifting my heavy pack, then started the long climb, wondering what the next hours would hold for us.

CHAPTER 52

The trail at first followed the creek that drained from the glaciers above. It was gradual and not at all difficult, even though we had to skirt a few big snowbanks.

Soon, we came to a big rock pile that provided unobstructed views of the Bugaboo Glacier above. It looked impressive, a vast and massive ice field with huge granite spires sticking out of it.

We now began gradually climbing, passing a beautiful waterfall thundering down in the late-spring snowmelt. We were soon on top of a moraine of glacial debris, and the views were spectacular. The towering spires were now more visible, and across from us was a forest of larches beginning to green up.

If I'd gone blind right after seeing that stunning view, I think I would've been OK, as I felt like I could never see anything that would beat it for perfection. It vaguely reminded me of the Cirque of Towers in Wyoming's Wind River Range.

I was doing fine, though tired and a bit weak, but we stopped often and rested and munched on gorp and chocolate. I swear I thought I saw something white in the trees several times, but it was elusive and fast moving. I wondered if one of the White Ones were following us.

Lisa also saw shadows, and we later decided we were probably being shadowed by more than one Bigfoot. It made sense, since a gathering had been called by Hap, and the big event would be the next night. There were probably Bigfoot everywhere around us, if only we knew.

I figured we'd gone about two miles when the trail really started to climb. This was the hazardous part we'd been warned about. I was beginning to feel winded and weak at the very worst time, as we were now to the steep part, where there would be fixed cables and a ladder to climb.

We started up a set of switchbacks. I was already flagging and my pack felt even heavier, and I had to stop and rest. As we rested, I could hear something or someone coming down the trail above us. They seemed to be making good time.

Just then, two young guys came around the corner carrying packs and ropes and climbing harnesses thrown over their shoulders as if they'd left without taking the time to really pack things up. They seemed startled to see us.

"Dudes," said a blonde guy who appeared to be in his 20s, "Or excuse me, dude and dudette, you might not wanna go up there."

He seemed a bit panicked and breathless. "I would definitely advise you to not go up there," he added.

"Why not?" Lisa asked.

Now the second climber, who could've been the first one's twin, spoke, "There's weird crap going on, chanting, loud voices, even something that sounds like booming, like pieces of glacier breaking off or something. We spent last night at the hut, and something tried to get in. We figured maybe it was a grizzly. We went ahead and climbed Pigeon

Spire, but on the way down something was throwing rocks at us, something really big and white, and that wasn't no grizzly. Man, listen, you do not want to go up there, trust me."

"I thought the hut was closed," I said.

"It is, but it isn't if you know how to get in," answered the second climber.

"How did you get in?" Lisa asked.

"The window on the right was unlatched, and we left it that way in case we would have to get back in if the Whatevers chased us."

"The Whatevers?" I asked.

"You'll understand if you go up there. Look, it's almost dark and you still have to do the cables, which is bad enough in good light. Just hike back down with us. We parked over by the lodge. You go up there, you die. Take my word on this one."

"OK, well, thanks for the warning. I think we need to rest here for a bit and think about things," I said. "You guys be safe going on down. Don't worry about us."

The climbers were soon gone, leaving me and Lisa there, and I have to admit I really wanted to go back down with them. I think Lisa guessed what I was thinking, because she just looked at me and said, "Packy, we can't let Hap down, OK?"

"OK," I answered, getting up and stumbling onward, but I didn't get far. My lungs were hurting, and I knew I was in no condition to continue. I had no idea what to do, so I sat back down.

And as I sat there, I realized the sun was setting and our precious daylight would soon be gone. I knew we had a

good mile or so to go, and it would be difficult in the dark,
even with headlamps, but there was no way I could get up
again. I was, for the umpteenth time on this journey, totally
drained and exhausted.

I sat and watched as the sun went behind a long purple
cloud, lighting its edges like the golden fringe on a shawl,
then sinking down until it came free of the cloud and again
shone on the horizon. It was now a huge gold-red orb,
lighting everything around it in a burnt-orange, like something on a distant planet.

And now all the granite spires glowed in the last rays of
sunlight as if they were lit up from within, and I knew then
why it was called the Place Where the Sun Lingers.

Soon, huge Moses rays broke through the clouds, making dark streaks across the sky, and the sun was quickly
gone beneath the horizon, just as a bat flew by us and was
outlined against it all.

I remember wondering why a bat would be up there in
the Bugaboos, but I was too tired to care. And just then, in
the opposite direction, I saw a full moon rising, a big gold-
en moon that took my breath away.

I wanted to be happy, to really enjoy where I was and
the stunning beauty around me, but I knew there was no
way I could go any further, and there was nowhere to stay
the night on that steep slope, and I felt like I had once
again let everyone down.

CHAPTER 53

Lisa and I just sat there on the trail, and she tried to make light of our situation, but it was impossible to feel anything but precarious, since we were truly in a precarious situation—not only because of the steep precarious mountainside we were on, but also because of the precarious company we were keeping—an entire Bigfoot tribe, I suspected.

Not to mention that we were both already getting cold. A person recovering from a pneumonia really might reconsider spending a night out at the foot of a glacier in the Canadian Bugaboos, I thought to myself, wondering what would become of me. Would Canada pay to have my body shipped home, or would they just leave me up here?

Lisa sat with her arm wrapped in mine, and I suddenly could feel her stiffen up. She put her hand across my mouth so I wouldn't say anything, and I knew she had heard something I hadn't.

Something was coming down the trail, something big and unconcerned about making noise, something that was maybe the king of the forest and thereby had no worries about its place in the food chain. Maybe something like a grizzly bear.

We quickly got up and scuttled everything back into the trees, trying to hide, but it was too late.

"I knew you'd come, Packy. I've been watching for you." It was Hap.

"Was there ever a question, Hap?" I cast back, as Lisa and I got up.

"No," he replied. "Hello, Lisa. I'm Hap, and this is my mate, one of the First Voices, who you call the White Ones."

Hap's mate cast, "I am Maxa, Glacier Lily. I hold your arm with good feelings in my heart."

Lisa and I both held our arms out to Maxa and did the arm grasping thing.

I then cast, "Hap, congratulations."

"Is good, Packy," he cast back.

"Hap, I can't go any further," I cast.

"I know, Packy. We carry you."

Before I could say siccum, Lisa was on Maxa's back and I on Hap's, along with our packs. And I can tell you, it was a terrifying experience going up those cables and that ladder on the shoulders of a Bigfoot. The exposure was tremendous, and we could see all too well in the moonlight.

I was relieved once we were on top at the Conrad Kain Hut, and even before we got there I could smell a faint musky Bigfoot smell, and I knew there had to be a lot of Bigfoot somewhere up there for the night to carry their scent like that.

Thinking of it gave me the chills, and I wondered what in the world I'd been thinking to go up there, to supposedly be the bearer of the Book of Runes, a book I no longer bore.

I knew I had to tell Hap that Tracker had the book, but I was afraid to. Not that I thought Hap would harm me, but

I didn't want to disappoint him, especially at this late date and with all his people there. But I had no choice.

We went through the window of the hut and left our stuff there, then Lisa and I stepped outside, where Hap and Maxa waited, Maxa's white coat shining in the moonlight. I recall thinking she was one of the most beautiful animals I'd ever seen, and Lisa later agreed when we discussed it.

"Hap," I cast with concern, "Tracker has the book."

"No, Packy, Nupqu the Teacher has it."

"Have you seen it?"

"Yes."

"Does it look like it got wet?"

"Yes, it's all wavy now. Nupqu says he got it from you."

I couldn't help myself—I started laughing.

"Hap, Nupqu has a fake, a book Lisa made. I threw it into the hot springs, and he must've retrieved it. It's not real. I mean, it's real enough, but not the real book."

Hap was silent for awhile, then cast, "Is real enough, Packy. The ceremony is tonight. We'll be back for you."

"Wait! Tonight? I thought it was tomorrow."

"We have it tonight. Everyone's here, and they're starting to fight over whether the book should be destroyed. We do it tonight or have what you call war."

Hap turned to go, but I cast, "Hap, I gave Tracker the real book. He may not even be here—he was seriously wounded when he shot himself in the foot and may be dead."

Hap stood for a moment and said nothing, then he and Maxa walked into the night, and I could see their shapes in the moonlight out on the Bugaboo Glacier with the huge shadow of the Bugaboo Spire behind them, and I recall worrying they might fall into a crevasse. It all seemed dreamlike.

Then Lisa grabbed my hand and took me back into the hut, where she pulled out her little backpacking stove and made us both a hot freeze-dried meal of cashew chicken, followed by a cup of hot tea.

And there we waited, wrapped in our warm sleeping bags, resting and waiting for the Whatevers to return for us, while I pondered Hap's statement that the fake Book of Runes was real enough, wondering if he had finally actually stopped believing.

CHAPTER 54

We waited as the full moon rose to the zenith, wondering if Hap would ever come back. We could hear chanting, and it seemed to get not just louder as the night went on, but somehow thicker, as if the night creatures themselves were joining in, the animals and insects and other inhabitants of the vast British Columbian mountain chain we were on.

I finally got up and looked out the window of the hut and could see a sea of huge creatures, the Bigfoot Nation, all together, chanting, and there, in front of them, stood Takoda, or Hap, their leader.

I thought of the Hap I had got to know as we trekked through the outback alone, wet and discouraged, even lost half the time, and was amazed at the depth of his character.

Takoda, Friend to All, leader of this leaderless group who had a leader only for major events that might occur once every fifty or hundred years.

And that night was one such event, for Hap had brought them all together from all over to destroy the old way, to destroy the book that had led to the near decimation of their tribe, the Book of Runes.

Finally, I saw Hap leaving the group and coming our way, along with two others.

"It's time, Packy," Hap cast.

I felt something I hadn't felt for years, something I can only describe as hope, though there was fear there, too.

I said, "Lisa, don't forget, you have the most important job of all tonight. I'll cast to you when it's time." She smiled.

Then Hap cast, "My friends Hamumu and Gwa'wina are going to stay here at the hut with you, Lisa, to make sure nobody bothers you, just in case."

Hap and I walked back to the crowd of Bigfoot, who seemed restless and even angry. The energy level was amazing, and I half expected the air to crackle with electricity.

Hap now stood in front of the crowd on a huge flat boulder and cast, "My friends, we will begin. With me is Packy, Bearer of the Book of Runes, who has borne the book all the way from the Rune Cave, far away, no easy task."

The Bigfoot roared, but I wasn't sure if it was in approval or disapproval. It was a sound so massive it started a small rockslide high in the spires somewhere across the Bugaboo Glacier.

A we stood and listened to the rockslide, Nupqu, the Teacher, climbed up onto the rock beside us, holding his Book of Runes, the fake.

He cast to the crowd, "I am Nupqu, Head Teacher of the Bigfoot Nation. I am your new leader. I hold in my hand the Book of Runes, and because nobody can hold the book without dying except your leader, it's a sign for you to follow me."

Nupqu held the book high in the air as everyone roared. He then shoved against Hap, trying to get him to step down, then cast to the crowd, "Takoda is a liar. He says the book should be destroyed, but the book is our light in the darkness and must be followed."

The Bigfoot were silent, but they seemed restless and tense. I was suddenly afraid, and I stepped back a bit behind Hap.

Hap cast, quietly, "Read to us from your holy book, Nupqu."

Nupqu blanched. Hap knew he couldn't read what was in the book, as it was in English, but Hap also knew Nupqu was a Teacher and would probably fake it.

And so Nupqu began, his casting gradually taking on power and strength, as he simply recited the things he'd been taught from childhood, things that were supposedly from the Book of Runes, things he'd taught many to believe, saying they were sacred tenets.

"Thou shalt obey the Teachers.

Thou shalt not befriend humans.

Thou shalt range across all the lands and keep moving.

Thou shalt not mate with any but your own color.

Thou shalt make fire and call it good."

Now a terrifying scream of anger came from the back of the Bigfoot crowd, and I knew immediately it was Tracker. Nupqu stopped, taken back, and I took advantage of Nupqu's fear.

I cast, "Look, friends, Nupqu's book, the old Book of Runes, was made by humans. Would you like to see what's really in it? Let me, a human, show you, then you can choose which book you wish to go by, Nupqu's or Takoda's."

I grabbed the book from Nupqu, who tried to hold onto it, but when Hap stepped towards him, he became afraid and let it go. I opened it, holding it out for all to see.

There, in all their glory, were photos of the Ice Hockey Greats of Fernie. I held the book open so everyone could see the photos as I turned each page and cast out:

"Jason Krog, center!

Bill Lindsay, winger!

Dan Smith, defense!

Shane Churla, winger!

David LeNeveu, goaltender!

Michael Teslak, goaltender!"

Now the Bigfoot all looked at each other, puzzled.

"See," I cast, "A book made by humans about humans for humans with pictures of humans. There was nothing there for you in the first place, it was all made up by the Teachers to keep you under their control. And through time, it got more and more entrenched in your thinking, making it harder and harder to revolt against. But these teachings are bad for you."

A murmur went through the crowd, and Nupqu slipped away, back into the rocks. And now I could see Chaska, Akecheta, and Tahatan, the Bigfoot we'd met at Blacktail, grabbing him and taking him away.

I continued, "And now, we look to a new Book of Runes, a new guide for our lives, one that will better serve all. Otaktay, are you here? Please bring the book."

I held my breath, hoping Tracker would come forward.

I waited and was about to give up, not sure what I would do next, when from the back of the crowd Tracker came slowly, still limping, but as he got closer I could see his foot was much better. He handed the book to me, then extended his arm, which I grasped.

"Thank you," he cast directly to me.

"You're welcome. I have a gift for you from Lisa," I cast back to him.

Tracker looked surprised.

"It's a new name for you—Wichapi, Star."

Tracker looked pleased, showing his teeth and nodding his big head sideways.

I then cast to all, "Friends, this brave Bigfoot, who is now called 'Wichapi formerly known as Otaktay,' is a loyal Bigfoot for bringing the new Book of Runes to us. He's a hero, for he's been seriously injured and brought it anyway."

Me and Tracker and Hap all knew it was actually the old Book of Runes, but I had a plan.

The Bigfoot Nation cheered, and Tracker seemed a bit embarrassed by the attention.

I turned to Hap and cast, "And now, I give the new Book of Runes to Takoda. He will read it to you. Read the new rules, Takoda, read from the new and reformed and heavily abridged Book of Runes."

Hap took the old beat-up book with much pomp, holding it as if it were made of gold, then opened it and began casting, supposedly from the book.

"Thou shalt follow your own counsel." (The Bigfoot all murmured, "That's good.")

"Thou shalt go wherever you want in freedom." ("Good, good.")

"Thou shalt befriend humans whenever you please." (Silence.)

"Thou shalt not range unless you want." (Clapping and shouting.)

"Thou shalt swim in warm lakes and sleep under leafy trees." (An enthusiastic "Good, good," with more clapping.)

"Thou shalt love whoever you please, whether of your own color or not." (Hand clapping and foot stomping.)

"Thou shalt eat pancakes!" (A huge shout like humans at a football game.)

After everyone quieted down, I cast, "And now, friends which book do you choose?"

A roaring came in unison, "Takoda's!"

Now I took the old Book of Runes back from Hap and cast to the crowd, "Let me show you, now that you've chosen this book, all the rules you must follow."

I opened the book and turned it towards them. There was nothing in it, no pages. The missing pages had each served us well as firestarter all the way from the Rune Cave to the Bugaboos, and now all that was left was the leather binding.

"See, there's nothing in it. It's empty. There are no rules, except those we carry with us internally, the rules of kindness and compassion and love for each other, and we no longer need so-called teachers to teach us, for we each think for ourselves."

The Bigfoot roared again.

And it was then that I knew what it was that had drawn me back to the Rune Cave and to the book—finally, I knew. Hap's journey, the journey he had taken on behalf of his people, it was also my journey.

Together, we had brought the saga to its conclusion, to the far end of the circle, and by doing so had created a continuum that provided a beginning and an end, a path of healing from all the many sorrows and wrongdoings.

It was then that I understood that my own life mirrored that circle, in that I had been both the creator and recipient of such wrongs, and it now was a thing closed in on itself, something completed and yet with a new beginning. I could take the new and make of it what I wished, just as Hap's people were now free to begin anew, to be who they needed to be to follow their own paths.

All the hardships, all the pain, it was all over, and such was the path of life. Hap and his people had that acceptance of things that we humans had long ago lost—they were like those who are truly a part of nature, they simply accept each day for what it brings and go on living.

And so, it was then, standing watching Hap now lift his massive arms and rip both books in half, that was the moment that I knew he and his people were free of it all.

And it was then that my anger dissipated, that my constant companion of grief and injustice fled, and I, for the first time in many years, felt a sense of elation, hope, and happiness. I knew Hap's people were free now, and somehow their freedom granted me mine.

I then cast, "And now, in closing, we humans would like to give the Bigfoot Nation a gift."

I cast directly to Lisa, over by the hut, "It's time."

Just then, the sky split in two, and a thousand stars rained down, stars of gold and silver and blue and red and green.

And the Bigfoot Nation at first stood in fear, but then a great cheering went up, one that could be heard clear down in the great Rocky Mountain Rift, in the towns of Nicholson, Parson, Castledale, Harrogate, Spillimacheen, Brisco, Edgewater, Radium Hot Springs, Dry Gulch, Shuswap— all the towns from Golden in the north down the rift to

Invermere in the south, although to those who stopped to listen it sounded like wind in the distant high mountains.

And then, Lisa set off another batch of fireworks, and the Bugaboo Spire and Howser Spire and the Houndstooth and Snowpatch Spire and all the big massive peaks were draped in a silver light, followed by a sparkling golden light that rivaled the sunset, though much shorter lived.

Now Maxa, Hap's mate, stood in front of the crowd and raised her hand until the crowd quieted.

"I am Maxa, and on behalf of my kin, the First Voices, I welcome you to the Nunataks. We will now party."

I left Hap and Tracker and made my way over to the hut, where Lisa stood with Hamumu and Gwa'wina. I thanked them and we grasped arms, then they joined their kind.

Soon, from where we were inside the hut, Lisa and I could hear what sounded like a huge xylophone, like bones striking bones, in a rhythmic and entrancing cadence that soon put us to sleep.

I awoke once to hear a loud chanting and the words, "Takoda! Wichapi! Takoda! Wichapi!" then drifted back to sleep, Lisa snuggled against my chest, and dreamt of a far away cave in my homeland and of a scruffy lost man who had once been me.

EPILOGUE

by Packy

After all was said and done, we went home.

I found out later that a small RV was found abandoned on the road to the Bugaboos, and three men were missing, all from the United States and affiliated with a Bigfoot research group.

I wondered if Tracker had anything to do with their disappearance—could they have been the ones trying to get the book? I guess I'll never know.

I also contacted the linguistics professor who I'd given the photos of the book to, and he told me they had deciphered the runes.

It was a journal of Erik the Red's travels all across western America into Canada, and had information about him traveling with several Bigfoot who were apparently his guides and led him into the Nunataks, the Bugaboos.

The prof badly wanted the book, as it was a major piece of history and very valuable, but I told him it was gone. Without the book, the photos weren't worth much, as people could say they'd been hoaxed. He was very disappointed, to say the least.

Lisa helped me sneak back across the border, dropping me off near the crossing at Polebridge. I left Wagger with her, snuck across, then hitched a ride down to Kalispell, where I rented a room and waited out the weeks it would take for my passport to arrive.

When it came, I called back up to Fernie and Lisa came and got me. She had a gift for me in celebration, a t-shirt she'd had made that said, "I've Never Been Arrested."

I had to laugh about that one, as I was sure she had no idea how many laws I'd actually broken. I'm not even sure I knew.

We were soon married, and I applied for dual citizenship, as did Lisa. It took awhile, but we were eventually able to live in either country, and so we ended up spending our time in Fernie and also in Glenwood Springs.

I opened a geology consulting business and was able to work from both towns, allowing us to pretty much come and go as we pleased. It was funny that both places had hot springs, which we often frequented, and both were located in traditional Bigfoot territory.

A couple of years later, Lisa wanted to go see the Rune Cave, so we went back to Coffee Pot Springs and hiked up into the cliffs.

To my surprise, all the runes had been destroyed. Someone had chiseled them off the limestone. I was too nervous to go inside, but I somehow suspected I would find the runes in there also gone.

But I did find a small piece of limestone on the ground with part of a rune on it, and to this day, I carry it in my pocket to remind me that I really wasn't crazy and that the whole adventure actually happened. It also reminds me of how lucky I was to find that cave and meet Hap.

And speaking of Hap, one day, a number of years later, along towards evening, I was sitting outside by the pond at our house in Fernie with little Wagger when I heard the sound of an owl. Wagger started wagging, and I knew it was Hap. He soon stepped from the shadows.

We grasped arms, and I can't tell you how happy I was to see him. Standing back a bit were Maxa and two beautiful Bigfoot children, both a creamy tan color. They came forward, and Maxa greeted me, then each child came and grasped my arm.

The first and oldest, a girl, cast, "I am Yaminqan, Bluebird. I hold your arm with good feelings in my heart."

The second, a boy, cast, "I am Little Packy, Bearer of Freedom. I hold your arm with good feelings in my heart."

I wanted to cry, but held it back.

I cast, "They're beautiful, Hap and Maxa, just beautiful. Thank you."

Hap cast, "We're on our migration, a journey to the Nunataks, a gathering to celebrate our freedom from the Book of Runes. I want to invite you and Lisa to come with us. You would be our guests of honor."

I thought long and hard, then cast, "Hap, I would love to go, but Lisa's out of town and I have to take care of things here. Give everyone my best, though, will you?"

Hap smiled, then I added, "Hap, I have something for you."

I went inside and got a large envelope and handed it to him. His big hands couldn't open it, so I opened it for him.

He took it and studied it for a long time, looking sad and happy all at once, if that's possible. I guess sad because it was the drawing of his Greats, and happy because

I'd torn it from the Book of Runes and saved it for him. He showed it to Maxa and the children.

"Packy keep as memory of Hap," he cast, handing it back to me.

"No, Hap, it's yours. Your kin."

"Packy, remember what it was like, wandering, sleeping in a nest, looking for food and water, every day? My life has no place for possessions. No place to carry it. It will get ruined, destroyed. Packy keep. Can put in box." He nodded towards the house.

"Thank you," I cast.

That picture now hangs above the mantle in our house in Fernie, that portrait of Hap's Greats, inside a beautiful frame of red cedar. It's the focal point of the room and also of many comments and questions. When visitors ask, Lisa and I just say, "It's a picture of another life, another time, and another world."

But now Hap and his family turned to go, and I stood there, watching as they then ran like the wind through the tall grasses, back to their kind, to the wilds.

And for the longest time, I struggled—I too wanted to go. I could smell the fresh rain on the wind and it called to me, but I finally turned and returned to my own kind.

AFTERWORD
by Professor Johnson

Since I'm the professor who was given the photos of the Book of Runes (as told in "Rusty Wilson's Bigfoot Campfire Stories"), I feel somewhat compelled to write this afterword. I've had many discussions with both Rusty and Sam (Packy), and as a professional linguist, I'd like to add my interpretation to this story.

Johnson is not my real name, and I hope you understand why I choose to remain anonymous. The world is full of those who would relegate the mysterious world of Bigfoot to myth, but neither Rusty, Sam, nor I are among those who do so, and sometimes it's best to not have people question your sanity, especially if your reputation is important.

I'm the only one of the three of us who has never seen a Bigfoot, but having read the original Book of Runes, I can assure you I'm now a believer.

As mentioned in the backstory, my graduate assistant, Roger (also not his real name) and I spent quite some time trying to decipher the runic characters in the Book of Runes, but with no success.

The runes were entirely unlike anything I'd ever seen, including Nordic runes, and I was totally baffled. They seemed to have no consistent pattern, and regularity of characters is a characteristic of all written languages, by definition.

We later determined they were boustropheden, where every other line of writing is reversed and the letters are mirrored. This is not uncommon in old manuscripts, such as the yet-to-be deciphered Indus script. With such documents, one must read alternate lines in the opposite directions, and this complicated matters greatly for us until we figured it out.

However, if it hadn't been for a lucky break that Roger had, i.e., his discovery of a possible Rosetta Stone of sorts for deciphering the characters, we would still be stuck, unable to decipher anything.

This break came in the form of an old manuscript from a museum in North Dakota, an old sun calendar with Siouan inscriptions written under runes.

Roger was later also sent a photo of runes with Siouan transliteration in a cave (not the Rune Cave, but rather a cave near Jewel Cave in South Dakota), but we now suspect that whoever inscribed them was doing so for religious purposes, as it appears they have no rhyme or reason. Perhaps it was someone who knew of the Rune Cave and was trying to emulate it. One of Packy's "Teachers" comes to mind.

But fortunately, we were eventually able to decipher the Book of Runes. Bear with me, as this gets rather complicated, and you can imagine how difficult it was for us to figure all this out.

Siouan was not a written language. At first it appeared that the runes were transliterated into Siouan using the Roman alphabet. In other words, someone knew the language represented by the runes well enough to translate it into Sioux. That person also knew English and used the English alphabet to represent corresponding Siouan phonemes as best they matched. So basically, we thought at first we had the runes translated from whatever language they represented into the Siouan language via transliteration using the Roman alphabet.

After some analysis, however, we discovered that the runes themselves were a written version of Siouan and we were really dealing with only one language that had been transliterated from one form of writing into another, from runes into an alphabet.

It becomes a bit complicated, but we engaged a Siouan language expert to help translate the text (with Sam's permission), and we were able to make sense of most of it, although there were often long phrases we couldn't understand. I suspected this was because such phrases were, like in the Viking sagas, kennings, which are the use of paraphrases instead of nouns. (One example is the famous Norse kenning "whale's road" for "ocean.")

It was my hypothesis that the Siouan speakers had thus been influenced by Norse speakers, and the original runes were indeed Nordic, but had changed through a long period of time. Why they became boustropheden is a mystery, as Nordic runes are not, but sometimes the religious use of a script will transform itself in such manners in an attempt to be more arcane.

The Siouan language in the text appeared to be an early version of Lakota Sioux, one that could easily have been only a couple of hundred years before the current version. Lakota Sioux is a well-studied and documented language.

After a good bit of analysis, we felt we had discovered a system that may have been an offshoot of the ancient runes used to write Old Norse, but that had evolved through time until it became a much different, though derivative, runic system used to record Siouan. But how did something with Viking influence come to be in the western United States?

As you may recall, the Vikings were active until about the mid-11th century, and in the story told by Sam, or Packy, the Bigfoot known as Hap states that his "Greats" brought the book to the Bigfoot Nation a mere 200 years ago, which would be long after the Viking era was over.

There has long been speculation that the Vikings were in the New World at least 500 years before Columbus, and such speculation was proved by archaeological findings in 1960 of a Norse village at L'Anse aux Meadows in Newfoundland that are over 1000 years old.

In addition, there is now mitochondrial DNA evidence of a Native American woman having been taken to Iceland over 1,000 years ago, leaving her unique genes in 20 to 30 percent of the current Icelandic population.

The settlement in Newfoundland is thought to have been founded by the famous explorer, Leif Ericson, son of the original Erik the Red, who had settled Greenland. Long before the Newfoundland find, many had noted Nordic features (fine boned facial features, blue eyes, blonde or red hair) in some of the Inuit people in these areas of Canada and Greenland.

Given that the Vikings have been proved to be in the New World, it's very possible that a descendent of Leif Ericson was the one called Erik the Red by the Bigfoot and was also the one who gave them the Book of Runes. This Erik the Red would have been many generations descended from the original Erik the Red who settled Greenland.

Thus, if the Vikings indeed brought their runic system to the New World, the period between when they arrived and when the Book of Runes was created would certainly be long enough for the runes to evolve into what we now saw in that book, and it is very possible that Siouan speakers adopted the system for their own uses.

It has also long been speculated that the Mandan tribe, who originally lived on the banks of the Missouri RIver but later relocated into North Dakota, were visited by a Welsh explorer named Madoc (or Madog) who married into the tribe and left his genes sometime around the year 1170 (that date approximated from oral histories in Wales).

Lewis and Clark noted the European features and red and blonde hair of some of the tribe's members, and the artist Catlin later visited the Mandans and painted a woman who could easily be European, yet was a Mandan native.

However, some anthropologists believe the Mandans were light-skinned and fair-haired not from Welsh blood, but from Viking interbreeding. One line of possible evidence is from an ancestral Siouan deity hero called "Red Horn," as well as early accounts of red-haired giants. Though the Mandans were enemies of the Lakota Sioux, both groups spoke variants of the Siouan language.

Was the Erik the Red of the Book of Runes somehow a descendant of one of the women of a Sioux group and a Norseman? It's my belief that this is indeed the case.

The Book of Runes turned out to be an epic account of the younger Erik the Red's explorations across the western United States and Canada. This in itself is amazing, as these explorations must have occurred some 200 or even 300 years ago.

One thing of note in the Book of Runes is Erik's mention of using several Bigfoot as guides. He notes that, as they traveled, the Bigfoot were friendly with the Native Americans and bore names from their languages.

But the real question throughout all of this is why Erik the Red would chose to burden the Bigfoot with his own beliefs, portraying it all as holy dogma sent to him from above in the form of the Book of Runes.

We do know from his writings that Erik was apparently a charismatic and persuasive figure and was able to successfully indoctrinate the Bigfoot into believing him.

Is it possible that these tenets were designed by him to try to help the Bigfoot? I believe this is where the truth lies, given the bit of history that we know.

For example, the tenet to not befriend humans could very well be founded in the fact that many Native American groups, in particular the Mandan, were almost decimated by smallpox brought by foreign traders. This could have provided Erik with a concern that Bigfoot not be exposed to human diseases.

And his rule for Bigfoot to range might stem from the same concern, coupled with the Viking value on individuality, as well as the fact that dispersal would make the group more resilient in terms of anyone being able to find them to kill them.

But why the maxim to interbreed only with your own color? Perhaps Erik had been through difficult times because of his own mixed blood. Who knows?

Given that the book was destroyed by the Bigfoot, and also given Sam's reluctance to have anything in our translations released (based on his own desire to protect these creatures), I have agreed it's prudent to drop the whole matter.

Sam has personally told me that his wish is for Rusty's book to present the evidence for Bigfoot as a way to increase our understanding of them, but to go no further with any proof of their existence. His reasoning for this is that he knows many things would change for them if such proof were presented, and probably not in a good way.

My feelings are that, even though the book could be carbon dated, no one would believe Erik the Red's descriptions of Bigfoot anyway. Without the actual Book of Runes, it becomes just a story, and it's possible that even with the actual book in hand, no one would believe, saying Erik was crazy.

In any case, it's been a long and interesting journey, one I feel fortunate to have been involved in, and it's certainly broadened my own understanding of the world around me in a way I can't begin to describe.

May the Bigfoot Nation live on in peace, and may we someday again become their friends.

THE END

ABOUT THE AUTHOR

Rusty Wilson is considered to be the world's foremost Bigfoot storyteller. Rusty has collected a number of Bigfoot stories from around the campfire, available as ebooks at yellowcatbooks.com and from your favorite internet retailer. They are also available in print at Amazon.com.

You can follow and communicate with Rusty at his blog at rustybigfoot.blogspot.com. And be sure to check out Bigfoot Headquarters at yellowcatbooks.com, where you'll find cool Bigfoot hats and koozies.

Also, you'll enjoy "The Ghost Rock Cafe" by Chinle Miller, a Bigfoot mystery, also available at the above websites.

Made in the USA
Lexington, KY
15 March 2013